LONDON CALLING

BOOK ONE

A Matter of
Trust

KAT FAITOUR

Want more?
Please sign up for free content and future books at http://www.katfaitour.com

DEDICATION

To Todd. For believing in possibilities. But most of
all, for believing in me.
And to Gidget.

Acknowledgements

Tamara Lush, fellow author and critique partner. Thank you for your generous spirit and gracious suggestions. Not only did you help me grow as a writer, but also you helped make this book better than it would have been. Again, thank you.

Bev Katz Rosenbaum for your early guidance and suggestions.

Editor — Megan Cavanaugh
(http://www.meganedits.com)

Cover design by James, http://www.goonwrite.com

CHAPTER ONE

Devon Sinclair never failed a test.

Job interviews were simply meetings between new people to determine whether a mutually beneficial relationship could be arranged. To be successful, one should be able to read those new people, determine their needs, and assess their preferences. Then one should establish oneself as a competent, even pleasing, solution. As a test, it was simple.

"Thank you for your time."

She stood, shaking the hands of each person on the interview panel before her. She was calm, even serene, as she followed each of them to the exit. She contained her smile to one of placid professionalism, fighting the grin that wanted to break free.

"Devon, we'd like to discuss a few things before we take you to lunch. We'll step out, but make yourself comfortable here for the time being. There's tea, coffee or any cold refreshments you'd like." The vice president of Human Resources waved a hand to a nearby counter before turning to leave.

Devon busied herself making an espresso before taking a seat. Crossing one long leg over the other, she swung it in a rapid rhythm before catching herself and tucking both feet beneath her. Looking around, she took in the stylish and sleek setting, appreciating the minimalist neutrality.

"External clutter promotes internal clutter," her dad would always mutter while clearing out any knick-knacks she'd accumulated before another move. Never one to be overly sentimental, he would add, "Keep the mind focused, Devvie. Clear out the fluff." She'd argued, but he'd been right, she supposed.

A clear head had gotten her to Sterling Enterprises interviewing for her dream job as one of their financial economists. And she had it; she knew it. All that remained was closing the deal with the top man himself, Bennett Sterling.

She smiled, taking a sip of darkly brewed espresso. A faint groan escaped her. It was the first coffee she'd had since arriving in London that was strong and bitter enough to suit her tastes. She lowered her head to inhale its toasted aroma, closing her eyes in ecstasy.

She barely had time to register the faint stir of air as a man hurried past to deftly place a small cup under the machine for a quick caffeinated double shot. Her eyes widened to take in the sheer breadth of him before registering his height. He easily topped out over six feet. He appeared absolutely solid and Devon leaned forward slightly, unconsciously anticipating how the rest of him might appear. For surely no one could be gifted with a face to match the rest. Shifting, she forgot her earlier poise and crossed one leg back over the other.

Hearing the movement, he startled, barely refraining from bobbling the small cup as he turned to see who was behind him.

He froze.

Devon didn't notice because she was too busy taking him in. He was all strong bones and lines, from forehead to jaw with only the faintest dimple in his chin to show any softness. Black hair waved back from his forehead where faint lines marked his age — somewhere in his early thirties, she guessed. But it was his eyes that arrested. Navy blue seemed too obvious a description, their intensity accented by sooty black lashes.

She shivered. And suddenly, she realized she was staring, and had been for quite some time. Heat flooded her cheeks and she briefly glanced down, tightening her hands on the armrests of the chair. She rose, extending her hand. "I'm—"

"There you are!" A petite blonde burst into the room. "I've been looking all over for you…" She stuttered to a halt, and then took a quick step closer, her mouth turning down when no one seemed to register her presence. Finally, she angled her body to interrupt their connection and firmly grasped the coffee cup loosely held in her employer's hand.

The man shook his head, before abruptly focusing on his personal assistant's agitated face. She tugged on the coffee cup once more before he released it, one black brow lifted in question at her urgency.

"We need to go. We're late." She snapped out the words, setting the cup down on the counter before turning to lead the way back out.

Devon's eyes traced him as he followed the other woman from the room. Just as he reached the door, he turned, and his navy eyes captured hers once more. He hesitated before turning to stride from the room.

***

Bennett's long legs quickly ate up the distance his PA was trying to put between them. Her gaze flicked upward as he easily moved beside her, and he swallowed a smile as her eyes narrowed in annoyance. Natalie Enfeld was a superior assistant, his operational right hand. One of her finer qualities was her ability to put people in their place.

His best strategy was distraction.

"Are all the files ready for the presentation? Did you go over the slides one last time?"

He nearly bumped into her when she abruptly stopped, just shy of the conference room where they'd be meeting with clients. "Bennett, I am hardly new at this. I have always checked the files and gone over the slides before every presentation for the last five years."

This time, he couldn't hold back. His eyes creased as a smile lifted the corners of his mouth in appreciation. "It never hurts to check, Natalie. No insult intended."

She returned his humor with a flat look. "None taken. But I believe I'm the one who should be concerned. You seem... *distracted*."

His smile slipped. He knew she was referring to his fascination with the other woman. He wasn't ready to dissect that, certainly not with his PA. He cocked his head, then shook it in denial.

"Not at all. I assure you I'm perfectly fine." He pulled open the boardroom door, ushering her in before him. "Let's do this. We still have a full day ahead of us."

***

As the meeting neared its close, Bennett finally allowed himself to drift. Not since Olivia had anyone taken his breath so. And yet, even Olivia hadn't caught him at first glance. He frowned, unable to remember the first time they'd met. Absently, he scratched his jaw, for once trying to call up the features he'd tried so long to extinguish from his memory.

He was blank.

No, not true. It wasn't Olivia, but he could still vividly see pale, flawless skin and barely tinted full lips. Regal cheekbones had flushed with embarrassment when she'd caught herself staring. Masses of dark, tumbling hair, pulled back into a clasp. He'd wanted to free it, plunge his hands into it, draw her toward him.

Her eyes had captured him — pale gray, nearly colorless. They'd swirled like fog in those moments, and he'd been sure she was as lost as he. Until Natalie's interruption, when he'd lost his concentration.

He abruptly straightened. He didn't know who she was. Not even her name.

He turned to Natalie, ready to make his excuses. As he opened his mouth, the building's power gave one brief surge then shut down into midday darkness.

And then the fire alarms went off.

***

Devon silently but sternly lectured herself in the bathroom mirror. How could she have stared like that? It wasn't as if she'd never seen a good-looking man before. Her best friend, Dominic Martin, was the closest thing to godlike perfection a man could get. They'd grown up together but she only saw him as a brother figure. Yet, she'd ogled a stranger like some hormonal fool.

She hoped, valiantly, she wouldn't meet him again. Everything had gone perfectly thus far; she prayed Sinclair luck would hold. And skill. She was here to prove that skill, hard work, and intelligence could go just as far. She nodded into the mirror, affirming herself.

Just then the lights shut off and the fire alarms sounded.

She looked up, casting an appeal toward the now dark bathroom's ceiling. "Okay, I'll take the luck. Some luck please."

Of course, nothing happened. She felt her way to the exit, gently pushing the door open. The hallway was shadowy but not nearly as dark, so she gingerly stepped out, looking around. There was no one, and she guessed everyone had evacuated or was doing so. The alarms rang, unabated.

Remembering her way, she continued to the elevators she'd taken earlier, knowing a stairwell must be nearby. Seeing the door, she cautiously approached, not sure what to expect. There was no smoke, no heat anywhere so far. She pressed her palm to the exit, reassured to find it cool.

Looking back, she was never sure what made her throw open that door so forcefully. But whether it was relief or panic, she gave it a shove, moving forward at a near run. Immediately, the door sprung back and she caught it before it could slam shut again. Muffled cursing followed an indistinct thud.

Pushing the door open wider, she peered around to get a look. A man stood, slightly stooped with one hand covering the lower half of his face, catching the blood that flowed in a steady stream from his nose.

She gasped. There would be no Sinclair luck today.

It was him.

***

For one insane moment, she considered turning tail and going back. But the alarms continued to shriek overhead and there was only one way down. Plus, the man was bleeding, obviously hurt. She touched his arm. Tentatively, she asked, "Are you okay?"

"Great," he gurgled. "Just *great*. You?"

Devon valiantly ignored his sarcasm. Anxious to see a bruise already blackening the area under one eye, she blurted, "Me? I'm fine! You're the one bleeding!" Practically wailing in distress, she added, "I think I broke your beautiful nose!"

Bennett blinked. She saw his eyes narrow, focusing on hers. He brought his hand down, and his blood was smeared across his fingers. Oddly, he grinned.

"No, actually, the woman on the third floor may have broken my nose when *she* shoved the door in my face. You just got it bleeding again when you hit me. But thank you for calling me beautiful."

Devon gaped. "You mean I was the second person to hit you with a door?"

"In the face. Yes, you were. But I must say I'm enjoying this go around much more." He leered suggestively, a smile crinkling the corners of his eyes. "Perhaps you'd kiss it to make it better?"

She couldn't help it; she burst into peals of laughter. Bennett took a step back but seemed to catch himself. Regardless, she couldn't stop. Several long moments later, she glanced up from where she'd half bent, clutching her sides. He stared back, clearly confused.

"*What*? What is so funny?"

Breathing deep to control the last rumbles of laughter, she replied, "You've had not one but two doors slammed into your face and you're *still* flirting. You should see yourself." Reaching up with unconscious familiarity, she brushed her fingers over his cheek before giving him a broad smile, inviting him into her joke.

Bennett captured her hand in his. "Have dinner with me."

Taken aback, Devon started to withdraw.

Talking fast, he added, "Well, first, let's get out of here. Then you can have dinner with me." As she continued to hesitate, he said, "After all, you smashed my beautiful nose. Then you laughed about it. Actually, you wouldn't *stop* laughing about it. So, my ego pleads with you to have dinner with me."

She wavered. Navy eyes locked onto hers and the world retreated, just as it had before.

"Please," he added.

She surprised them both by saying, "Yes. Okay." She stopped, knowing she was in danger of babbling. She had no idea what was wrong with her, but this man flustered her beyond belief. Suddenly, she remembered, "But I don't even know your name."

Bennett smiled. "Let's work our way downstairs, shall we?" He gestured a hand for her to precede him and Devon realized the blasted alarms were still sounding off in a shrill cadence.

"We can cover all our personal details along the way, just promise you'll let *me* get the doors from now on," he teased.

She giggled, completely charmed. They sped down the stairs while he tossed rapid-fire questions to her, all trivial and light.

"Zodiac sign?"

"Scorpio," she answered.

"Mm, dangerous," he said. "Favorite color?"

Vivid, extraordinary navy invaded her mind. "Green, but I'm not Irish. I'm part Scottish."

"Hmm, but which part?" At her laughter, he continued. "Dogs or cats?"

"Both!"

He made a rude buzzing sound, like she'd missed a question in a game show. "Wrong answer! You have to choose."

She thought of the little figurine she'd managed to smuggle away from her father's rabid decluttering efforts. Real pets had been out of the question. "Fine," she said, eyes bright. "Cats."

"Favorite wine?"

"Sancerre. I'm part French." She heard him stop, and looked back.

"That explains your features. You should thank your parents for striking genetic gold." She paled slightly but before he could ask, they reached the exit to go outside.

Bennett moved ahead to open the door and Devon went out, stepping onto the sidewalk. She turned, about to finally ask his name when several people swarmed, nudging between them. Even at nearly six feet in heels, she struggled to see over their heads to find him.

The repeated call of, "Mr. Sterling, Mr. Sterling!" finally caught her attention. The fact that everyone seemed to be shouting towards him made her abruptly pull back. *Oh no, it couldn't be.*

The crowd parted to give Devon a glimpse. He was standing next to the petite blonde from earlier that day when he'd been getting espresso. Devon watched as the other woman dabbed at the blood on his face. Then she straightened his tie before reaching up to brush one unruly lock of hair back from his brow.

Devon felt a tightening in her chest. There was a certain intimacy in the woman's actions that left her feeling foolish and exposed. She cleared her throat, glancing around for some kind of escape. A nearby firefighter caught her eye, all too eager to help. He came over, explaining the alarm was false so everyone was safe to return to the building.

She turned, unsure. With a strangely thick throat, she walked back into the building. Some would have considered it an impossible situation.

She straightened her spine, increasing her pace. No, not her. She thought of her goals and dreams, her plans. And they did not derail at the first obstacle, even if it was a man who'd taken her breath away — the first man ever to do so.

No. When she met Bennett Sterling later in the day for her personal interview, she would forget she'd ever shared those moments with him in the stairwell. Or looked into the intense navy of his eyes.

Devon Sinclair would not fail this test.

CHAPTER TWO

BENNETT CURSED AS HE WATCHED his mystery woman walk back into the building. He knew she'd seen Natalie fussing over him; the crowd had parted before their eyes locked. Hers had lowered in hurt or dismissal, he was unsure. But he was certain, somehow, that she wouldn't tolerate such scenes. His voice clipped, he answered the officers' questions about the site.

He was losing time. Like a fool, he hadn't gotten her name when he'd had the chance. Now, she'd gone back inside, but he had no idea where. And *who was she?*

He froze, unease snaking up his spine. Raking a hand through his hair, he tried to recall if any of his employees were American, likely from the South considering her slight accent. He couldn't place any, but Sterling International was a large company with hundreds of employees. It was possible he might not know her.

Maybe she was contracted; a temporary staff member hired from another financial firm. But it was best to know outright. He moved to go back into his building when he saw the fire chief approaching.

Bennett clenched his teeth, giving the man a hard smile. He had to take care of the chief's questions, but impatience was making him quick-tempered. Reluctantly, he summoned his PA.

"Natalie. I need you to find the woman that came out of the building with me. Tell her to wait so I can talk to her."

Her eyes slightly narrowed. "Certainly. Is there anything else I should ask?"

Treading carefully, he replied, "Yes. Her name. And find out where she works in the company."

She walked off to do as he asked, her posture rigid. Bennett watched until she disappeared back inside the building, regret knotting his belly. She was reliable, a trusted confidante. He'd never seen her as anything more, relieved to find a woman he could work with in platonic harmony.

Except he'd been careless, too self satisfied to notice when her feelings began to change. Now, he'd sent her after a woman who'd captivated him in one afternoon. A woman who may well be an employee, someone he'd have no right to come near, especially after the disaster with Olivia. He pinched the bridge of his nose, sighing.

What a damned mess.

***

Natalie searched the lobby before walking to the elevators, frustrated. She had neither the time nor inclination to comb the entire building for Bennett's missing woman. But he'd made the request and she always did what was asked of her. Visitors, consultants, and contracted staff could be anywhere. The woman had definitely seemed professional, similar to the hundreds of financial experts that populated Sterling International. So, where was the logical place to start?

Natalie remembered the scene she'd walked into earlier. Bennett and the woman had been consumed with each other, unaware anyone had even walked into the room. She'd looked on as he ran his eyes hungrily over the other woman's face, as if memorizing every contour. Uncomfortable, she'd interrupted them to pull him away.

That had occurred in Human Resources. What if the other woman was here to interview for a position with the company? Natalie thought back, remembering how the woman had been seated, as if waiting. She couldn't remember what she'd worn but had a vague impression of polished style. She'd been young, but certainly old enough to have her degree and work in any number of departments. She might already be an employee; just not one Natalie had met.

A slow smile tilted the corners of Natalie's lips.

Bennett Sterling never dated employees. Not ever. She should know.

Taking a deep breath, she felt some of the tension leave her shoulders. Unhurried, she stepped into the elevator and punched the floor for Human Resources. If she was right, things were about to get interesting.

***

Natalie looked around, seeing no one in the department. Was anyone ever here? Earlier, it had been empty, save for Bennett and the other woman. Now, it seemed to be void of any life again. She huffed out a sigh, turning to leave when she ran into Aidan, one of Bennett's favored directors.

"Aidan," she exclaimed. "I'm glad I've found you. I need to postpone a meeting you have scheduled with Bennett later this afternoon. He has an interview with a new candidate and wanted more time with her than I originally allotted, for some reason." She glanced around, seemingly distracted. "I have no idea where everyone is, do you?" She flicked her cuff back with a manicured finger, checking the time on a slim, gold watch.

"They'd be with the new candidate, probably the one you're talking about," he answered.

She looked up, finally giving him her full attention. "Is there just the one? The one Bennett is interviewing later?"

"Yes, I'd guess that's her. She's quite the big deal, has everyone pretty worked up around here. I have to say I'm eager to meet her, it's why I'm here."

She paused, noting the excitement brightening his brown eyes. She raked her gaze down, seeing he'd dressed up more than usual, donning a sport coat over a white shirt and knotted tie. "Who is it? What makes her so special?"

"She's probably the smartest economist Harvard's produced in a decade, and that's saying something. London School of Economics wants her, will probably get her, but if we can employ her in the meantime, it would be a feather in our cap. She's going places, that's for certain. We'd like her to take us along." He paused, taking a breath and looking around Natalie to see down the hall. "I can't wait to meet her."

"You make her sound like some wunderkind. Does this paragon have a name?" Natalie forced a laugh before pressing her lips together. How could anyone be *that* perfect? But if it were the woman from earlier, Bennett would *have* to hire her. Good grief, Aidan made her sound like she was the economist of the century, practically woman of the year.

Natalie paused, her brow smoothing out. If Bennett hired her, there would be no more lingering looks, no pursuit. He was a man of rules. His first and foremost was never mixing his personal life with business. He never made exceptions, not as long as she'd known him. There had been rumors of a woman once, from long before, but he'd never spoken of her and she'd never asked.

She looked over at Aidan, realizing he hadn't answered. He was still looking down the hall around her, but suddenly turned to meet her eyes.

"They're back from lunch. It's my turn to meet her, do I look okay?"

He motioned to his tie and she nodded her approval while inwardly marveling at his enthusiasm. This was a man known for his calm demeanor under pressure. Aidan Kennedy was unflappable. He was also happily involved with another woman. Yet here he was nervously primping and fussing over some stranger.

Men.

She turned, ready to see this ideal of economic wizardry that had everyone leaving their posts and changing schedules, including Bennett. Her eyes met and locked onto another's, ones of a nearly colorless gray.

Natalie Enfeld smiled, triumphant.

***

Bennett knew his worst fears were realized as soon as Natalie returned. She walked up, shoulders back, with a satisfied gleam in her blue eyes.

"I've found her," she said. "And there was no need to ask her to wait or bring her round." She paused, expectant.

Taking the bait, he replied, "Yes? Why would that be?" Impatient with her, he snapped out, "Why don't you get on with it, Natalie? Who is she?"

Chastened, she answered, "Because you're already meeting with her. *She* is Devon Sinclair." At Bennett's silence, she continued, "The financial economist interview candidate? You're meeting with her a little later. You asked me to block out more time than usual, remember?"

Bennett remembered.

She was the most promising economist to hit the job market in years and there was fierce competition to get her. He had no doubt about his company's ability to attract and retain talent. Sterling International was one of the top financial investment firms in the country, if not the world. They were small and niche, but ultra successful. Their clients were guaranteed privacy, discretion, and they'd delivered top monetary returns for decades. Their reputation had skyrocketed since Bennett took the reins in his early twenties, a maverick with an eye for risk that paid big dividends.

Unless something was fatally flawed in her personality, she was guaranteed the job. He knew London School of Economics also wanted her and he was willing to work around her schedule if need be.

Anything was up for compromise. Anything to get her.

He met Natalie's gaze. Her brows were slightly raised and the satisfaction from earlier was gone, replaced with a question. "Yes?" he asked.

"Her day is packed up with interviews, meetings and tours. Human Resources didn't leave her much down time. But I can carve something out for you. Would you like that, Bennett?"

He touched her arm, knowing what it had cost her to ask. In this at least, he could reassure her.

"No. There won't be any need for that. I wouldn't want her to get the wrong impression."

He turned, missing the relief that briefly flashed across Natalie's face. He stepped into his office and moved to close the door.

She stopped him, worry etching her voice, "Bennett."

"Yes?" He was suddenly tired. The solace of being alone beckoned, even if it was for a few snatched moments.

"Aidan seemed so excited about her, this candidate. From everything I heard things are going extremely well today with her interviews. Do you think you'll hire her?"

His shoulders tensed, his hand tightening on the edge of the door where he held it. He looked over his shoulder back at Natalie.

"I suppose so," he replied.

There was a dullness in his chest and his arms felt heavy as he closed the door behind him. With a little luck and good negotiation, Sterling International would gain an incredible asset soon. As CEO, he should be elated, victorious.

Instead, all he felt was empty regret.

***

Later, Devon would marvel at the fact that she'd gotten through the day, let alone been hired on the spot.

She'd attended her meetings and interviews, toured the building. As the time for her interview with the man she knew to be Bennett Sterling had neared, she'd been keyed up yet resolved. She was determined to get the position. It was everything for which she'd worked, studied, and sacrificed. She would not let a moment of confusion, insanity really, make her lose sight of what mattered.

She needn't have worried.

Gone was the man whose gaze she'd fallen into. Gone was the man whose trivial questions had charmed and amused her as they'd galloped down the stairs while alarms jangled overhead.

Instead, she'd met Bennett the CEO, president and heir to Sterling International. He'd been cool and professional, as if they'd never met at all.

Which was just the way she'd wanted it. Absolutely.

And she'd gotten the job of her dreams, another checked box on a list made years ago. Back then, she'd decided to be different, and do differently than her father and business partner, beloved as they were to her.

She certainly wasn't disappointed when she found out she'd be working directly with Aidan Kennedy, one of Bennett's top directors and his Chief Financial Economist. No. In fact, it was a *relief* to find out she wouldn't have to see Mr. Sterling so often as she'd feared, given their initial associations.

She was definitely relieved.

So, it was a mystery why she had to swallow hard against the sudden tightness in her chest when he'd informed her. In one breath, he'd offered her a generous employment contract, and then told her the position wouldn't liaise directly with him.

"You'll work with Aidan, my Chief Economist. I believe this will be a better fit all around and lead to the best outcomes for both you and the organization." He'd spoken with authority, not quite meeting her eyes.

In fact, he hadn't met her eyes at all. Not once since finding out who she was.

"Yes, of course. Thank you for this opportunity. And I look forward to working with Mr. Kennedy. We got along quite well during my interviews."

Bennett looked up sharply, but she'd already been moving forward to hold out her hand. She'd pressed her lips tight, waiting as he hesitated. Then, he'd firmly clasped her hand in his larger one.

And it had all begun again.

It was if an electric current passed between them, one to the other, impossible to say with whom it originated. She'd jerked her hand away, foggy eyes locking onto shocked navy before breaking away to look down. She'd backed up one step, then another as she'd pressed a hand, hard, to her heart. Muttering something polite, hopefully business appropriate, she'd groped for the door and fled before losing the job she'd just gained along with any dignity she had left.

If she'd stayed, she might have seen Bennett pressing his own hand to his chest too, before leaning back in his chair with a bitter smile.

CHAPTER THREE

AFTER SEVERAL WEEKS, DEVON BEGAN to relax. Aidan had a way about him that made her feel like a peer rather than a subordinate. In fact, he cleared up any misconceptions regarding her status early on.

"Devon, I'm the Chief Financial Economist and one of Bennett's senior directors here. As your supervising manager, I'll assign projects and oversee your work. But this isn't an old-fashioned hierarchy. You'll be part of a team that operates as equals. We're all excited to have you come on board."

She gifted him with a broad smile, which seemingly robbed him of speech. While aware of her beauty, she was largely oblivious to its impact.

"That's so nice of you to say. And such a wonderful way to lead. I'm very happy to be here."

He stared back at her, blankly. Her smile slipped, replaced by puzzlement. Finally, he shook his head, squared his shoulders.

"Right. Let's get you started."

That had been the beginning. Aidan was everything he promised to be, assigning projects that met her expertise then stretched her knowledge. She was autonomous, which signaled trust. She couldn't have asked for more.

Meanwhile, Bennett Sterling became a ghost. He drifted somewhere near the peripheries of her existence. If she entered a meeting, he'd leave. If she exited, she'd later hear that he came in after. Occasionally, she stepped into the elevator and caught his scent. It was darkly spicy, the woods after a rain. And always, *always*, she was catapulted back into the navy abyss of his eyes.

She caught herself looking for him, straining to hear the deep bass of his voice. Seeking him. If she didn't know better, she'd think she missed him. Of course, that was ridiculous. She didn't know him. But all in all, it was stretching her nerves.

Devon Sinclair was never nervous.

She nearly shot out of her skin when she looked up one day to find him seated across from her. "You scared the life out of me!" Breathing hard, she placed a hand on her chest and nervously laughed. "What can I do for you?"

"Well that's *one* way to bring some color to your cheeks," he said blandly. Devon could feel her face getting even hotter as his gaze slipped down, following the line of her neck. Unconsciously, she glanced down, checking to see that her buttons were all done up. She looked up to see his eyes creased with suppressed laughter.

Was he *flirting* with her?

Flustered, she snapped, "Is there something you actually want? Or did you just stop by to scare me, or toy with me?" Horrified, she clapped a hand to her mouth, dropping her eyes. She'd overreacted, caught off guard by seeing him after weeks of absence.

"Really, Devon, I had no idea you had such a mouth on you." Steepling his fingers, he stared while she fidgeted in the uncomfortable silence. She was never unprofessional, no matter how provoked. Until today.

Finally, he spoke. Tapping the papers in front of her, he said, "That report you're working on? Be ready to present it by 8 a.m. tomorrow. My team needs the data to make decisions on an investment I'm considering. They'll meet with you in the boardroom. Don't be late."

At that, he rose to walk out of her office, leaving her to consult the watch on her arm to see that it was already late afternoon. Picking up the phone, she dialed Aidan. They were in for a long night.

***

Bennett took the private elevator back to his office suite. It was reserved for his use and that of special clients, those requiring high levels of privacy and security. He rarely used it himself, preferring the same services and facilities as those of his team.

But he needed a moment.

It had been a tense few weeks since Devon came to work for him. He'd avoided her, congratulating and telling himself it was for the best. Then, he realized it was unnecessary. She was just a woman. One among many.

He chalked up his reaction when meeting her as an aberration. Too much work, too little sleep, or some combination. He needed a night out, a date with any one of the women he had listed in his phone's contacts. He was certain he'd call one of them soon, any day.

He told himself all of that while he made his way to her office, an area from which he'd steadfastly kept away. And he told himself he was immune until he stood staring at her in the doorway, momentarily stunned anew. She worked on, unaware of his presence. Taking a seat, he clasped his hands before she could see their fine tremor.

He was caught a bit off guard. He tried to put them both at ease with some light conversation, but he certainly wasn't flirting with her. She'd been wrong to be rude. He had no intentions toward her; he was merely being friendly.

He walked out of the elevator, pausing by Natalie's desk.

"What's on my calendar for tomorrow morning, first thing?"

"You have a video conference with the Leeds branch. You'll be talking to your directors there."

"Cancel it. Reschedule. Clear my time from eight to nine. I'll be attending Aidan's presentation in the board room."

Natalie's eyes narrowed. He knew she was aware that Devon was leading the project. He normally never attended project meetings, preferring to hear the summaries from his directors with their recommendations.

But he sometimes made exceptions. Of course he did.

***

It was brutally early the next morning when the incessant ringing of her phone jarred Devon awake. Blearily, she fumbled before answering, "Hello?"

"Dev! Top o' the morning to you, lass!" Devon winced as Dominic Martin's voice boomed out his greeting.

"Dom," she sighed. "You know I'm in England. Not Ireland. And please lower your voice," she groaned while fumbling to sit up amongst her covers. Tucking the phone between her ear and shoulder, she folded her legs to keep covered in the chilly morning air.

"I see someone still isn't a morning person. Late night, sugar?" Dominic purred in the gravelly voice natural to him, with a hint of an American South accent.

She blinked at the bedside clock, trying to bring it into focus. "*Yes.* We didn't finish up until after 2 a.m. Is it *4:30*? God, why are you calling me at 4:30 in the morning?" She started to tip sideways back into bed.

"Well, it wasn't to hear your chipper voice," he snarked. "No, I'm waking you up to share good news. I'm coming to visit. Looks like I'll be coming to London a little later this year. How's that for a good reason to get out of bed and start clearing up?" Dominic knew Devon's interests lay in spreadsheets and books, not cleaning and dusting. They always joked she worked in an organized state of disarray.

Wide awake, she froze in the act of swinging her legs to fully sit up. "That's… wonderful. Why?"

There was a quick beat of silence. "Dev? Why do I get the impression you're not happy? Is something wrong?"

Devon loved her family. Dominic Martin and his father, Patrick, were no less included in that group than her own father. She'd joked about having dual parentage, alternately raised by her dad, then Patrick and his wife Alice when she'd still been alive.

But now Devon was determined to make her own way, on her own terms. A lonely desire to see her closest friend and surrogate brother warred with fierce independence. Love won out. "No, Dom. Everything is great, other than being crazy busy. I may not have all the time I'd like to spend with you, that's all. But we're flexible, right?" She paused, hopeful she hadn't hurt him with her hesitation. "I'm glad you're coming. I didn't think you'd be able to with your workload."

"I have an opportunity over there that I'd rather look into sooner than later." Dom had started his own tech software company some years ago and was hugely successful. Recently, he'd expanded the business into security and personally designed firewall systems to help keep his clients' information secure.

"Ah, so the real reason emerges!" She laughed, relieved. "I'm glad to hear that, actually. I would have worried you'd be bored here. My hours can be a little brutal at times." She thought of last night's marathon. "But if all else fails, I'll bring you to work with me. I bet Sterling International could use some of your security software, right?"

She was only half kidding. They took great pride in each other's work. Perhaps there was an opportunity for him in Sterling's rarified world of investment banking. Caught up in her thoughts, she missed his own pause.

"Ah, well, we'll see about that. Dev, listen, someone's at the door. It's probably my dinner being delivered. I better go."

He abruptly ended the call. Devon stared at her phone before switching it off. By her calculations, it was 10:30 p.m. in Chicago, a late supper even for Dominic. Shaking her head, she thought it far more likely a female friend had arrived at his door. Chuckling, she rose.

She missed him. She scooped coffee into a French press, pouring in hot water from the kettle she'd boiled. He'd help her get her bearings back. This *thing* with Bennett, whatever it was, had unsettled her.

Dominic helped her remember herself. He always kept her centered; this would be no exception. And in return, she would pursue some introductions for him.

She headed for the shower, balancing her coffee on the sink basin so it could cool off. She'd ask Natalie, Bennett's PA, if she might help acquaint him with some key contacts.

Surely, the woman would cooperate. While she hadn't technically warmed to Devon in the past weeks, she had thawed a bit. Besides, Dominic could charm the birds from trees.

Satisfied, Devon thought no more of it, moving her mind to work. Even after her late night and interrupted morning, she buzzed with energy. She couldn't wait to get back and show off her work to Bennett's directors. It was almost a shame he wouldn't see it.

***

Four thousand miles away, Dominic Martin sat in the penthouse suite of his Chicago high-rise, surrounded by glass and steel. He sipped the Jameson he'd poured while talking to Devon, grimacing as it burned down his throat. He deserved a little pain, lying to her that way.

He rolled his neck, working out the stiffness. No, it wasn't lying. He just wasn't telling her everything. He would keep a few secrets, for a little while. Tossing the rest of the whiskey back, he swallowed before setting the glass down, hard.

He opened his laptop to read the file he'd started on his next client.

Bennett Sterling.

***

Talking with Dominic left Devon upbeat. As she walked to work, she felt confident and ready. She'd dressed in a crisp white shirt and navy pencil skirt, tucking peep-toe heels in her bag to slip on later while wearing ballet flats for the commute. She'd tied back her thick brunette hair with a bold geometric scarf. Simple, chunky gold jewelry finished the look.

She kept positive right up to the moment when she looked up from preparing her notes, ready to begin. Bennett sat at the boardroom table, directly in front. Swallowing, she glanced at Aidan to see if he'd noticed.

He approached with an encouraging smile. Laying a hand on her shoulder, Aidan leaned close. "It looks like we have unexpected company. Don't be nervous, you can do this. Just explain the information we have. And be yourself." He gently pressed her shoulder with his fingers, then took his seat.

Across the room, Bennett's eyes narrowed at the fleeting exchange.

Clearing her throat, she began, "Ladies and gentleman, as you are aware, we've recently completed a Chinese Yuan valuation study. I'd like to present our findings."

Forty-five minutes later, Devon sucked in a shaky breath while smiling at Aidan in camaraderie. The presentation went overlong when Bennett fired rapid questions about the data, research, and prospective market changes. Tempers frayed as his interrogation strayed into demands for predictive future stabilities.

Aidan snapped, "For God's sake, how could we possibly know that? You don't want market analysts; you want us to be clairvoyants."

Devon caught Aidan's eye to slightly shake her head in warning.

He continued, "And frankly, you could take things a little easier on Devon. She's doing very well and her presentation included all the information you asked for." He smiled in reassurance while she inwardly cringed.

Bennett slid his gaze from Aidan to Devon. A muscle bunched in his jaw, but he took a deep breath, visibly loosening. Leaning forward, he braced his forearms on his knees. "Mr. Kennedy, I pay you, all of you, to know the world markets. You are not merely market analysts. You're some of the best economists working today. I should know. I found and hired you." He leaned back, at ease and in full control.

"Let me remind you what economists do, Aidan. They predict the future. And if they're wrong, they explain. But my economists aren't usually wrong. You're the best. Being the best includes providing more than what's required. Or *requested*."

He swung his attention directly to Devon. She was riveted by the intensity of his stare.

"You'll learn to anticipate what I need, and you'll give it. Do you understand what I'm saying?"

"Perfectly." She kept her eyes trained on his, refusing to be intimidated. Plus, she dreaded looking at anyone else to see if the sparks and innuendo were as apparent as she feared.

As if sensing her disquiet, Bennett was up and out of his seat, signaling the end of the meeting.

"And that's why he's the boss." Aidan stepped over to help her collect her things. "I know that was tense, but he thinks you're doing very well. He's always positive when we review your progress." At Devon's puzzled look, he continued, "He's asked for regular updates. I assume he wants to ensure you're settling in, adjusting to things here."

On one hand, she was relieved the tension with Bennett had gone unnoticed. Aidan seemed genuinely unfazed, obviously not hearing any double entendre in Bennett's words. Perhaps she shouldn't either. Frowning, she focused on the conversation.

"Is that usual? For new staff?"

"Well, no. But honestly, I want you to be happy here too." He gave her an awkward pat before holding the door for her to step through.

Devon walked through to find Natalie and Bennett standing directly in front of her. Aidan, hard on her heels, bumped into her back, jostling the files and laptop she was carrying. Quickly coming to the rescue, he saved her from dropping it all by grabbing her arms to steady her.

"Whew! That was close." He reached in to straighten her load before clasping her wrists in shared relief.

Bennett and Natalie stood motionless, never moving an inch. Natalie raked her gaze from Aidan to Devon, smiling coldly.

"This is cozy. I hope we're not interrupting anything, Aidan."

"No, of course not. And I think you know that, Natalie." His voice held quiet dignity.

With that concise declaration, he won Devon's friendship. She beamed at him in approval. Natalie interrupted them with a pointed look at Aidan's hands, still resting loosely on Devon's wrists. Aidan flushed, removing them immediately.

"He was helping me. I almost dropped all my things," Devon rushed to his defense.

Bennett's voice cut through the conversation coldly. "Devon, be in my office in fifteen minutes."

***

Precisely fifteen minutes later, Devon walked into his office suite, stopping in front of Natalie's desk. Knowing the other woman heard Bennett order her to be there, Devon stood silent. She suffered the other woman's mute survey, waiting as Natalie's gaze traveled down and back up before meeting her eyes. Devon matched her slight smirk with placid indifference. Seconds ticked by.

With resolute nonchalance, Devon asked, "Shall I take a seat?"

A flash of respect darkened Natalie's pale blue eyes. Pasting on a false smile, she answered, "No, Mr. Sterling is ready for you." She rose to open the door to his office.

As the door was closing behind her, Devon heard her add, "*Good luck.*"

***

As soon as she walked in, Bennett knew he was doomed. It was too soon after watching her talk on about money markets and futures for nearly an hour while he'd struggled to focus. Her beauty had seized him from the time she entered the boardroom. But her brain had him equally smitten. She was faultless and brilliant. It was too bad he'd probably only heard a fraction of what he needed to know.

Did she affect everyone the same?

Aidan had blathered on, defending her like a medieval champion. Aidan, a senior director best known for being cool and self-possessed. A man also known to be seriously involved with an attractive and likable young woman.

Looking around, Bennett's entire team of directors had been glued to Devon, riveted. She was fascinating and compelling.

To everyone.

He waved a hand to the seat directly across from him and waited as she crossed to it. His temper pulsed through him as he took in how she squared her narrow shoulders, facing him. She sat straight and upright, crossing her ankles beneath her chair.

"Devon, are you aware of this company's policies regarding workplace harassment?" He kept his tone cool, to match her bland expression.

"Yes." She offered nothing more, and he inwardly seethed. Her expression assumed mild expectation mixed with patience.

"And are you aware that Aidan Kennedy is a happily involved man, soon to be engaged?"

"No."

Goaded by her lack of emotion, he burst out, "And do you *care*, Ms. Sinclair?"

She smoothed her skirt, glancing down at her hands. "No, actually I don't." Her eyes lifted and he was startled to see they'd darkened to deep charcoal.

"It has nothing to do with me. Mr. Kennedy is my managing director and we don't share a personal relationship." She leaned forward to lay a finger on the edge of his desk, subtly pointing at him. "If you're implying something else, you're wrong. *And* you're out of line."

Her calm announcement was paramount to setting a match to gasoline. Bennett smacked a palm down on his desk, rocking her back in her seat while clearing his own head of her nearness.

"You've got some cheek coming in here and telling me I'm out of line in my own company, Ms. Sinclair."

She paled but didn't shrink back further. "I resent the implication that I'm some femme fatale intent on seducing your male employees away from their faithful partners." She added, "Frankly, it's insulting. And baseless."

"Dammit, I didn't imagine everyone's reaction to you in there, Devon." He saw confusion flash across her face before she blinked it away. Frustration at her composure gnawed at him. He continued, glaring, "Let's drop the pretense, okay? It's not as though I haven't experienced your charm firsthand."

Satisfaction raced through him as her mouth dropped open to quickly shut again. Spurred on, he continued. "The only surprise today was seeing you in action around everyone else. You bewitched and entranced every man in that room today. It was *quite* a performance." He bit out the final words with savage precision.

They found their mark. Devon reared back, her face leeched of all color. Her eyes widened and pained hurt arced from her to Bennett. Suddenly, his anger fell away, leaving him confused and conflicted.

"Dammit, don't look at me like that!" He growled the words, scraping a hand over his eyes to block her from his sight. He couldn't have imagined the effect she was having on everyone this morning. He *couldn't*.

Determined, he looked back at her. She'd folded her arms across her abdomen, tucking her hands into her sides. She still sat straight as an arrow, but he had the impression she'd withdrawn somehow. Her eyes looked through him, beyond him, and were back to being a nearly colorless gray.

"Devon," he began again. And he almost missed it, so intent he was on what he was about to say. But she winced, nearly imperceptibly. He surged up from his chair, but halted when she flinched, more obviously this time. He started to reach for her, then hesitated, unsure.

Tonelessly, she said, "Are you firing me?"

Shocked, he overcame his resistance and lightly touched her arm, quickly removing his hand once he had her attention. He sat down again, leaning back with his hands laced over his abdomen. "No, Devon. I'm not firing you." When she looked back at him, blankly, he repeated himself. "I'm not."

Bennett didn't know what the hell he *was* doing anymore. He'd been angry; he'd needed to hurt her, vent his frustration at her. But when he'd looked past himself to see her, wounded and tucked into herself, he only felt hurt himself.

But damn it, he hadn't sent her away from him just so she could beguile another man. And he *hadn't* imagined her effect that morning on Aidan and the rest of his team.

"Devon, I'm not firing you. But I'm switching things up to keep an eye on you. You'll work under me now."

***

Devon refused his bait. She was wrung out and wanted to leave his sumptuous office with its miles of plush carpeting and darkly paneled walls. She also wanted her job. She'd worked too hard and for too many years to get here. She wouldn't toss it all away on temper. And he hadn't *hurt* her earlier; she'd been caught off guard, that was all.

She inhaled, taking a deep breath and relaxing the tension from her shoulders. She smoothed her skirt, then clasped her hands to keep them still. She would not give him a fight, no matter how he goaded her.

"I'm happy to serve Sterling International in any capacity you think best." She also wouldn't use his incendiary terminology. Working *under* him? She nearly laughed at his bold outrageousness.

Bennett arched a brow. "Good. You can meet me here, early, say six-thirty on Monday morning." She merely smiled at the early time, not raising a word of protest. He continued, "In the meantime, I want you to hand off any projects to Aidan."

That caused a pang for Devon, knowing she'd be leaving work that mattered to her unfinished. Plus, Aidan had his hands full with his own workload. Taking a gamble, she made one attempt at reason. "It would be easy enough for me to finish some of my work out, Mr. Sterling. I could work weekends if you're worried it would interfere with your own projects. Maybe Aidan would come in too if I needed him."

Bennett's eyes narrowed and a muscle bunched in his jaw. "No, I forbid it. You're missing my *point*. I'm not worried about your damned projects. You have enchanted Aidan, and I won't have it." He pinched the bridge of his nose, before continuing in a low tone. "He's a good man, involved with a good woman. I will not see him waste that on some misguided infatuation with you."

"So your solution is to move me up here?" She waved a hand to encompass the elegant surroundings. "Am I to sit at your side, like a puppy? Or perhaps you'll put me with Natalie, your PA? Am I to file your folders and organize your calendar?" Her voice rose in outrage as she continued, unabated. "Are you suggesting I do your *paperwork*?"

Bennett shifted under the directness of her stare. "No, of course not and stop being ridiculous. But you're moving to my team, like it or not. I mean it, Devon. I saw what I saw today." He flushed under the dark tan of his skin and abruptly straightened, pushing his shoulders back.

Devon inwardly cursed herself for allowing anger to sneak through her defenses. She looked down at her ringless fingers, collecting her thoughts. But no matter how many deep breaths she took, the fact remained. She was coldly, murderously furious.

She faced him, guileless. With a slight smile, she asked, "And what makes you think *you'll* be immune, Mr. Sterling?"

Rising from behind his desk, Bennett came to stand at his full height of six feet four. Devon's insides jolted at his expression, but she remained motionless as he walked around to lean back on the desk in front of her. He reached down and, grabbing both armrests, pulled her chair closer to him until they were practically touching knee to knee.

"Oh, I'm not immune, Devon. I've made my attraction clear to you already so it would be disingenuous for me to pretend otherwise. Besides, you are quite beautiful, not to mention intelligent." He reached down to lightly cup her jaw. She was surprised to feel that his fingers were slightly rough on her skin, as if he didn't spend all his time sitting behind an executive desk. She forgot to pull away as she stared up into his beautiful navy eyes, nearly missing his next words.

"But I see now I wasn't special. I suspect you've left a devastated trail of men behind you, Ms. Sinclair." She thought she heard a tinge of bitterness in his words, but it was gone as he continued, "Maybe you've left someone in America. Are you lonely?" His thumb absently caressed her skin, coming to rest in the small cleft of her chin. "Is it simple company you miss, or the pleasure a man can bring?"

Bennett couldn't have been more off the mark. Devon involuntarily grinned, conversely pleased at his wholly inaccurate description of her. She had friends, male and female, but kept them all at a comfortable distance. Her background, and her family, didn't allow for close relationships. With a burst of humor, she wondered how he would react if he knew she'd never had a lover, American or otherwise.

His fingers lightly tightened, wiping away her smile. "Something humorous about that, Devon? Or perhaps it's me you find funny."

Before she could react, he raised his other hand and cradled her face between both wide palms. He flexed his thumbs to tilt her chin up further before leaning down and placing his mouth over hers. Shocked, she felt the unexpected softness of Bennett's lips press into hers. One of his hands tunneled into the thick waves of her hair while loosening the scarf she'd tied there. A gentle nibble caught her full lower lip.

Surprised, she looked straight up into his watchful gaze. Rising from the desk, he took one hand and pulled her up from the chair to stand within inches of his body. She felt boneless and heavy, languidly acquiescent. He took advantage by lowering his lids and meeting her mouth again, deepening the kiss while his other hand slipped back to cup her face. She placed her hands on his shoulders, unsure if she wanted to push him away or pull him in. Her hands relaxed as the delicate pressure of his tongue slowly caressed the seam of her lips. She opened her mouth on a sigh of pleasure.

Bennett took his time exploring. Nipping out to press kisses and teasing bites along her neck, she heard him breathe deeply. With eyes barely slit open, he cruised his lips across her exposed collarbone, having pulled her blouse away as he feasted on the soft skin. Whimpering, she tugged him to bring his mouth back to hers. But he ignored her, pulling at her loosened hair to sting her into submission.

She opened aroused, stormy eyes onto midnight blue. Bennett braced a strong arm to the small of her back and pulled her more fully up against him. His other hand gently flexed on her jaw, opening it more fully before his mouth slanted down in dominant passion.

Their tongues danced in a silken duet, each searching and finding its mate. Devon's nipples pebbled against the lace of her bra and she instinctively pressed herself closer to the hard wall of his chest, hoping to ease their ache. He flicked the tip of her tongue with his and she moaned, feeling a hot rush of arousal. She linked her hands behind his neck, pulling him in, seeking relief to the tension assailing her.

He gentled her, smoothing his hands down her spine in a soft caress. When his hands reached her waist, he pulled her slender hips into his rigid hardness.

Devon sighed, lost in pleasure. She'd never been seduced, certainly not only with a kiss. But the taste and feel of him was new, warm, and exotically different. His solid maleness was a perfect foil to her fine build; a groan escaped her as she appreciated how flawlessly they fit.

She pushed her hips in harder to cradle the thick shaft of his erection. Gripping his shoulders, she attempted to widen her stance, cursing her tailored skirt. Bennett apparently sensed what she needed. Circling both hands around her bottom, he lifted her against him. Devon felt his length ride up against her as he thrust his hips forward, his tongue mimicking the motion within her mouth.

She carelessly coiled one foot around his calf as her skirt rode up mid-thigh. When her pump thudded to the floor, Bennett twisted her around, bumping aside various items as he placed her bottom on the edge of his desk. Pressing closer between her legs, he hitched up her skirt and exposed the lace bands of her stockings. He grazed his hand along her thigh, playing with the elastic before withdrawing to her knee.

Devon was impossibly immersed in him. For the first time, she understood the lure of passion and what it was to crave the sturdy strength of a man over and around her. So it took a moment for her to register the sudden tension in Bennett. She opened her eyes to see him staring back in stunned surprise. She was shocked when he leapt back, tugging her skirt back into place and bringing her knees together. Gripping both hands to help her from the desktop, he righted her when she stumbled against him, imbalanced by standing in one shoe.

She stared down at her missing pump, drunkenly lying on its side from where it had fallen earlier. Befuddled at the quick turn of events, she stared at it in dumb silence. She licked her lips, feeling their swollen tenderness. Glancing up, she saw his were reddened as well.

Bennett's jaw tightened before he abruptly sat her down in the chair she'd recently inhabited. He held out the errant pump, waiting for her to take it as she was still staring at it, bewildered. Finally, she looked up and his harsh expression froze all the previous warmth from her insides. A high pitched laugh escaped, and she said, "Is this my Cinderella moment?"

He shoved the shoe at her, where she fumbled to accept it with numb hands. "Don't be a damned fool," he grated.

Stung, she replied, "Relax, Bennett. I'm hardly expecting a proposal."

There was a brief but brittle silence. The bitterness she'd glimpsed in him before was back, this time in full force. "That's good, because you'll not be getting one from me now or ever. Much better than you have tried and failed."

The long fuse of Devon's temper vaporized. She'd rather be damned for pride than mistaken as some silly girl. With the light of battle firing her eyes, she neatly flipped her pump around before letting it fly like a dagger, straight toward his face.

CHAPTER FOUR

SHOCKED, BENNETT ONLY JUST MANAGED to palm it. Holding the high heel tightly, he demanded, "Just what the hell was *that*?"

"That's my shoe. Now give it back so I can have another go at your ignorant, insulting mouth!" Fairly glowing with anger, Devon flew off the chair to grab at the pump.

Bennett snapped upright, holding her shoe overhead out of reach.

"Give it to me! Give it to me right now, or so help me God, I *will* hurt you!"

"Devon, calm down." His words had the opposite effect on her already skyrocketing temper, but he nonetheless repeated, "Devon, I said *calm down*."

Chest heaving, she stepped back, but violence sparked in her soot-dark eyes. Unbelievable, he thought. No one would compare the collected persona she normally presented to the vibrating tornado before him.

He sat down beside her, motioning her to join him.

"You're making a mistake and you're going to regret this. Now calm down. You essentially just assaulted me. Do I need to remind you I'm your employer?"

Devon sat, but continued glaring. Her voice was deadly when she finally spoke. "First, I want to assure you that I am entirely calm. So, you can stop talking to me like I'm some hysterical female."

He started to interrupt, but she silenced him with a single finger. "And you are an arrogant, ignorant baboon of a man if you think I'm going to regret a single thing I'm about to say."

Bennett opened his mouth, then snapped it shut again as she continued.

"I'm only going to say this once, so try not to interrupt me again." Eyes flashing, she went on while Bennett sat and listened, seething. "You kissed *me*. Yes, I participated but you initiated. I enjoyed it, but that doesn't mean I'm here to seduce you, or anyone else, for that matter. Frankly, after listening to you now, I wouldn't have you on a damn platter."

"Are you *finished*?"

"No, I'm not." He couldn't believe it as she continued to rail at him. "Finally, you're *not* my employer because, as of right now, I *quit*."

With that, she leaned forward and grabbed her shoe out of his unsuspecting grasp. He was left staring as she slipped it on and walked out, never looking back.

***

Devon lied. By the next morning, she was fairly eaten alive with regrets. *I've ruined my life. I've ruined everything my Dad and I worked so hard for, all because I lost my temper.* Sitting on the sofa in her flat, she stared around her at the simple, but cozy décor. She had a place for herself here, seeing the odd pieces she'd brought home, making the space her own. *And now I've ruined it. How do I stay in London without my job?*

She checked the time, deciding it would have to do. Reaching for her phone, she pulled up the familiar numbers and pressed the button to dial. Within moments, she leaned her head back on the couch as the call connected.

"Dad? It's me, Devon." Pausing, she added, "No, everything's *not* okay. I messed up. Do you have a minute?"

John Sinclair never failed his daughter. Her eyes bright with unshed tears, she heard her father say the words she needed.

"Devvie, I always have time for you. Now tell me what's wrong."

***

Across town, Bennett tried to explain to Aidan Kennedy that Devon wouldn't be coming in.

The other man questioned, "But why? We had plans to finish this valuation study. Is she sick? You know what, I'll go to her place and check on her. She's alone here in London. No family." Before he could leave, Bennett stopped him with a firm hand on his arm.

"Aidan, she's not sick. She resigned."

"*What*? No, that can't be right. She wouldn't do that. This job meant too much to her. There's been some misunderstanding."

Sighing, Bennett released his arm. "I'm not sure she was the right fit."

"Not the right fit? Are you kidding me? She already caught us up on projects that were backlogged for a month. She's a genius, Bennett. We couldn't have *designed* a better fit."

"Sure you're not letting personal feelings cloud your judgment, Aidan? You sound like her damn protector."

Considering, Aidan replied, "I'm starting to think she might need one."

"Listen, I'm not going to let some new employee walk in here and wrap my team up in knots. I didn't like the vibe I got yesterday."

"What? So now she's gone?"

"I told you, Aidan. *She* quit. I didn't fire her. So, put your sword away."

"You know, Bennett, I've worked for you a long time, and known you longer. But I have never known you to be irrational or unfair. Right now, you're being both. And I have a feeling that doing so lost us the best team member we had." Shaking his head, he walked to the door, and turned back to say, "You're wrong about her. And you're wrong about your staff. You should have given us all more credit."

Bennett was rapidly tiring of other people walking out after getting the last word in. He rubbed the corded muscles of his neck in a quick massage. Reflecting on what Aidan said, he came to a decision.

"NATALIE!"

Despite being summoned by a shout through the walls, she appeared in his doorway, unruffled. "Yes?"

"Get me Devon Sinclair's address. And clear my schedule for the rest of the day."

***

Devon hung up the phone with an action plan. Her father hadn't placated her with empty assurances that everything would be fine. Instead, he'd listened while she talked. He hadn't pressed for explanations, but encouraged her to focus on solutions to her current problem.

What's done is done. Move forward.

For that, she was grateful. When he'd asked if she wanted him to fly over to help, she declined. She needed to fix this for herself, especially as she'd most exceptionally broken it.

The buzzer interrupted her thoughts, and she unfolded herself to see who was calling.

"Hello Devon." Bennett seemed to enjoy her surprise. "May I please come in?"

Instinctively, she glanced behind her to see if everything looked okay. When distracted, she got messy.

Following her look, he asked, "Unless I'm interrupting?"

With no sign of effort, he catapulted her from relaxed to irritated. He *would* assume she was entertaining. He must think she was some sort of man magnet. Honestly, she'd been in London for weeks, not months. Who would she have met?

"No, Mr. Sterling, it's just us." At his look of satisfaction, she added, "It's too bad, since you'll be quite alone with me here. Your reputation could be compromised. Then what will we do?"

Her words didn't seem to have the desired effect. Coming close, Bennett's lips curved in a slight smile as he lingered in her space a beat too long. Her breathing quickened as she stepped back, and he moved away to the sofa where she'd been seated.

He asked, "May I sit?"

She hesitated, but curiosity won out. "Certainly." She moved a stack of papers onto a near table and asked, "Tea?"

"That would be nice, thank you." He settled himself in, looking for all the world as if he were planning a lengthy visit. She shot him a glance, narrowing her eyes before leaving the room.

She performed the now common ritual of boiling water and preparing tea. After giving herself several minutes, she brought it back into the sitting room, balancing it on the low table in front of the sofa. The nearby armchair was stacked with files and books, as well as her laptop where she'd been researching other London financial firms.

She poured both their cups and offered accompaniments before impatiently taking the only other seat available next to him on the sofa. She eyed him expectantly. "How can I help you?" She kept her tone polite. Despite her earlier regrets, she still felt raw from their last meeting and her insides were a quivering mass of nerves.

Bennett took his time savoring the tea before pronouncing, "This is quite good."

The man was impossible. "You don't have to sound so surprised. It *is* merely tea, you know. The British don't have some monopoly on it." A flush started to warm her cheeks, but he interrupted.

"Now, before you reach for a shoe, I come in peace."

Astonished at the humor crinkling his eyes, she stared. Finally, she let loose with a reluctant chuckle, followed by a throaty laugh. "Oh, all right! I'm sorry. You've discovered my fatal flaw."

At his inquiring look, she announced, "I hold a grudge."

Barking with laughter, Bennett relaxed back into the sofa. "It's good to know you *have* some flaws. I spent the better part of the morning being dressed down by Aidan. He fully informed me about your utter perfection and how wrong I was to let you escape." He reached out a hand in invitation. "Truce?"

She considered his hand before slowly taking it. "Truce." She was relieved to put some of the ugliness of yesterday away. "Although we won't be seeing each other any more."

His hand tightened fractionally on hers. "That brings me to the reason for my visit. I'd like you to reconsider your decision to leave the company." He shifted forward, meeting her gaze squarely. "Devon, I want you to come back."

Involuntarily, she glanced over at the now empty table where she'd stacked her CV and other notes. Her eyes darted back to Bennett's.

He waved a hand containing all her documents. "Forgive me. I was just looking them over while you made the tea. I hope you don't mind, since I've seen them previously."

She couldn't refute that. They'd been in her application to his company. "No. But why are you looking at them now?"

"Devon, I made mistakes." He pointed to her CV. "This reminds me how large one of them was. Come back to Sterling International and I'll make certain you don't regret it."

"What do you mean?"

"I can offer you stock options and bonus incentives," he paused, letting her ponder the bait.

"An apology would cost less."

"Excuse me?" His brow lifted in puzzlement, replacing the pleased contentment from moments before.

"You could apologize. It would be cheaper, but perhaps not easier." A muscle in his jaw tensed. She hurriedly continued, "You admitted you made mistakes — in the plural. What else?"

He shifted to set his empty teacup down on its saucer. Leaning forward, he suddenly seemed closer in the small, shared space. "Kissing you. I overstepped the boundaries of our professional relationship. If you return, it won't happen again." He hesitated and added, "I don't date staff. It's a personal rule with no exceptions."

Devon blinked. Hurt from his comments caught her unprepared and she visibly swallowed.

He continued speaking, seemingly unaware of her distress. "The offer stands. You can take the deal or leave it, but I do have other places to be."

Devon rapidly remembered how the day had started and how much she'd wished for another chance. "That's fine with me, Mr. Sterling. I'll take your deal. And you can keep the apology."

Bennett narrowed his eyes before giving a short nod. "I'll expect you back in the office tomorrow morning."

Devon nodded in return, not trusting herself to speak. Things had gone far more in her favor than she could ever have hoped. Yet, she was wary, feeling like prey before his watchful gaze.

He rose to leave. "I do have one condition, Devon. If I hear you refer to me as 'Mr. Sterling' just one more time in that prissy tone, you won't have to quit, because I'll gladly fire you myself."

She stood, astounded, as he turned and quietly shut the door.

***

Devon walked to work the next morning with frowning deliberation. With rapid and long strides, the scenery passed, unnoticed. She needed to gather herself, prepare for what lay ahead, while putting to rest what lay behind.

After Bennett left last night, she'd quietly rejoiced in having her job back. But with the threat of eminent disaster averted, she had time to revisit that *other* evening. Before tempers had flared, passion flamed.

She tried to rationalize.

It was only a kiss. Albeit a good one, but still only a kiss.

Sighing, she struggled with honesty.

Good? If that kiss had been hotter, I'd have caught on fire.

Hearing friends discuss their love lives over the years had given her a jaded if amused view of relationships. She felt superior for avoiding the drama of soaring lust followed by swift and certain heartbreak.

Logically, it was probably an ordinary kiss, by most standards.

She quashed down the uncomfortable twinge in her stomach. Now was not the time to think about Bennett Sterling. It certainly wasn't the time to think about his mouth or how it had felt on hers and the way he'd kissed down the length of her neck. No, she wouldn't think about any of *that*.

She greeted Aidan before dropping off her bags in her office. Within minutes, she was debriefing statuses, handing off work, and catching up from yesterday's absence. An hour later, she stopped him, breathless. "So, you're taking on all my projects?" She hadn't considered Bennett would carry out his plan to change her work structure, especially not after what happened between them.

Aidan looked at her blankly before understanding settled on his face. "You haven't been told. I'm sorry, but you're moving." He paused to clarify, "That didn't come out right. It's not bad that you're moving." He swallowed, taking a breath. "You'll be working upstairs with Bennett. We'll still liaise, too," he assured her. "But this is an excellent opportunity."

She moved on autopilot. Stepping off the elevator with Aidan, she stopped in front of Natalie's desk. Bennett's door was firmly closed.

Natalie looked up without raising her head. "Yes? May I help you?"

Devon had an insane urge to say, "Reservation for Sinclair. Desk for one." Instead, she settled for glancing between the boxes she and Aidan carried. "I've been asked to move my workspace. Where should I take my things?"

Natalie didn't answer, just rose, disappearing into Bennett's office while Devon and Aidan were left standing awkwardly. Several minutes passed until she reemerged, walking back to stand beside them. "Follow me."

Entering her new office, Devon stopped and stared. Like Bennett's, it was tasteful and elegant, but much more feminine. Olive carpet anchored the room while a midcentury blonde wood desk kept the space modern. She trailed her hand over a matching bookshelf, turning to Aidan and Natalie.

"This is gorgeous. I couldn't have designed an office better suited to me." She beamed her pleasure.

"That's good to hear. Bennett just had it redecorated." Natalie interrupted Devon's admiration of a stunning oil painting of a London street scene, complete with bright red buses.

"Oh, I see."

"He likes to redecorate the offices and main spaces periodically. It keeps things fresh."

Devon quickly dismissed any ideas that Bennett might have personally chosen everything for her. She smiled weakly. "That's very good of him."

"I'll take the compliment." Bennett interrupted, surprising all of them in the doorway where he lounged. "For what exactly am I being praised?"

Devon blushed, inexplicably tongue-tied. Aidan looked at her and spoke up.

"Everyone is admiring your good taste." He raised his chin, indicating the general surroundings.

Bennett pressed a finger over his smiling lips. His eyes never left Devon's. "I'm glad you like it. I picked it out with you in mind."

Devon's heartbeat quickened. She forgot about the other people in the room, seeing only Bennett and his beautiful midnight gaze.

Natalie cleared her throat. "Well this is all very cozy. But perhaps we should get on with things?" She pointedly eyed Bennett before moving to the door.

Bennett lingered for another second, leaning slightly towards Devon as he maintained eye contact. Then, shaking his head a little, he turned to his PA.

"Of course." Frowning at Natalie's obvious impatience, he swiveled back to Devon. "It's good to have you here. Please unpack, settle, and then meet with me to go over your new responsibilities."

He walked out, leaving Natalie to follow.

***

Hours later, Bennett yanked off his tie and unbuttoned his shirt as he walked through his Notting Hill townhouse. Trading his suit for dark denims, he added an untucked button-down in soft cotton. Barefoot, he padded down to his kitchen.

He eyed the sterile solitude. Cool marble and stainless steel surrounded him as he gathered ingredients for a simple salad and omelet. His mobile phone lay on the counter, full of female contacts.

He tore romaine with more vigor than necessary. As he lined up ingredients for vinaigrette, his thoughts were of two women in particular. Combined, they were enough trouble for any man.

First, Natalie was moody.

They'd worked together, seamlessly, for over five years. She was integral to his success, both personally and professionally. He winced, thinking of the times he'd joked about her being his other half.

It had been too easy to begin partnering with her at occasional social engagements. They'd never progressed to being lovers, but he realized now she had feelings for him that he didn't share. Sighing, he admitted it was another miscalculation on his part.

Because that was all before Devon.

He drizzled olive oil into the dressing while he whisked. Since that first, fateful day, Devon Sinclair had enchanted, enraged and consumed him. He absently rubbed at the tension knotting the muscles in his neck.

He needed to take back control.

The kitchen door opened behind him, admitting a tall, silver haired man. Wiping his hands on a towel, he embraced the older man.

"Granddad." He fielded his coat, hanging it on a nearby peg. Handing his grandfather a spoon, he said, "Taste this. Tell me if it needs anything."

Charles Sterling pronounced the vinaigrette superb while perching on a stool at the large work island. He reached for the open bottle of Chablis sitting nearby and filled the two glasses Bennett slid toward him.

"I've been thinking of paying you a visit. You beat me to it." Bennett raised his glass, acknowledging the older man.

"I can still beat you at most things, despite my age." Laughter brightened his grandfather's dark-blue eyes. "I'm certainly better at socializing. So tell me what you're feeding me, then catch me up on everything else happening with my favorite grandchild."

Bennett lit the burner under the small omelet pan, watching as a pat of butter sizzled into foam. He rolled his neck and chuckled, realizing all the tension had gone.

"You're getting wine, salad, and an omelet, in that order. Maybe a brandy later since you think you're so funny." He turned, sliding a perfectly rolled, airy omelet onto a warm plate before passing it to his grandfather. "I'm your *only* grandchild."

***

Later that evening, Bennett sipped cognac in an overstuffed armchair situated at a right angle to another containing his grandfather. Fire flickered in the fireplace close by. "I'm glad you stopped by."

Charles swirled his brandy, examined, and then breathed it in before taking a drink. With eyes closed, he said, "Mm. As usual, you have excellent taste. Of course, you come by it naturally." Eyes crinkling with humor, he enjoyed another swallow. "Now tell me what's bothering you. Business or pleasure?"

Bennett briefly considered prevaricating. However, he knew his granddad would see through him and dig his heels in further. Bennett pinched the bridge of his nose, choosing his words. "I suppose it's both. There *is* a woman. *And* she works for me. She's smart, beautiful, dynamic. She's also driving me out of my damn mind."

Charles listened, completely relaxed in his chair, cognac lightly clasped in one hand.

Bennett continued. "Obviously we can't have a relationship. You know how I feel about dating within the company," he broke off at his grandfather's puzzled look. "You must know I never do after Olivia. That was a disaster." He took a breath then said, "This would be worse. Olivia was a mistake, there's no disputing that." He met his grandfather's kind eyes and said, "But Devon Sinclair would be my downfall, Granddad."

Years ago, Charles Sterling had founded and built Sterling Enterprises into an empire that his grandson later expanded. He was as sharply astute as ever.

"I never realized how profound Olivia's effect was on you."

"I'm not jaded," Bennett explained. "But it was a hard lesson and I prefer to learn from my mistakes. Olivia only did what was natural. She decided I wouldn't be her best bet, took a better offer." He shrugged; the pain from that old betrayal still stung. "I haven't been angry with her for a very long time."

"No, but you've let it dictate every relationship since. It's shaped you and how you see people." Charles paused then said, "Bennett, you were hurt. You made rules to avoid that same situation. But rules don't really save you from pain, and you might miss out on a person that makes it all worth it."

Bennett wrinkled his brow, thinking. "Was Gran worth it? Even knowing you'd lose her too soon, would you do it all again?"

"I'd do it a thousand times again. A day with Rose was worth a hundred without her," Charles replied firmly.

Bennett was awed by his grandfather's devotion, even after all this time. He raised his glass, signaling a toast. "To Gran," he intoned, clinking the crystal.

His granddad eyed him over the rim. "Now tell me about Devon Sinclair. Would Rose have approved?"

Bennett frowned. "I'm not so sure about that."

Charles questioned, "Why?"

Bennett ran a hand around his jaw. "She threw a damn shoe at me," he confessed.

His granddad burst into gales of laughter. When he showed no signs of stopping, Bennett ruefully shook his head, refilling their glasses.

He should have kept that to himself.

CHAPTER FIVE

"ONE MIGHT BE FORGIVEN FOR thinking this is a kidnapping."

Devon good-naturedly teased Bennett while secretly enjoying the excitement of being whisked away in an Aston Martin by a sexy six-footer with midnight eyes and ebony hair. The sun was shining, it was a gorgeous spring day, and she was in London. She decided to ignore the fact that he was her boss.

He flashed a grin before turning back to his driving. His strong hands were capable on the wheel of the low-slung car that effortlessly devoured the miles to their destination. Of course, she had no idea what their destination was, but couldn't drum up any real curiosity. She surveyed the intimate luxury of the car's cockpit, wide-eyed.

Absentmindedly, she caressed the smooth leather of the seat and armrest while eyeing up the man next to her. *Could he be any more gorgeous?* Dark hair curled just to the collar of a navy suit that nearly perfectly matched his eyes. He'd left off a tie today, wearing a pristine white shirt with the first few buttons undone to reveal tanned brown skin with the suggestion of curling dark hair. Swallowing, she took a deep breath and inhaled the woodsy cologne he favored. A sucker for such things, Devon exhaled on a sigh.

"Everything okay?"

Bewildered, she looked over into concerned blue. "What?"

"You made a sound. Like a groan. You're not ill are you?"

How humiliating. Never one to dodge a bullet, Devon faced the squad. "Oh. No, that was just me embarrassing myself." At his inquiring look, she explained, "You smell really good. I mean, I love scents. Cologne, perfume, flowers, candles. You name it. Whatever." Rambling to a finish, she sealed her lips and looked out the window.

The silence was oppressive. Devon risked a glance and Bennett was face forward, seemingly focused on his driving. Miserably, she apologized. "That was awkward. I'm sorry but you asked and I was just being honest." When he remained quiet, she added, "I'm not being forward or flirting with you.

You smell good. That's all." She looked down to inspect her manicure, her face flaming.

After several long moments, he finally spoke. "It's okay, Devon. I'm flattered. I have it on good authority that I have a beautiful nose, too."

Relieved, she looked over to return his smile but faltered, seeing that his didn't reach his eyes.

Changing the subject, he said, "Tell me how things are going. You've been with us for a while now, mainly working with Aidan. How goes it?" He was cool, like when he spoke to staff in a boardroom meeting.

The small confines of the car no longer felt intimate but restraining. Devon looked out the window, not seeing the bright sunshine any more. Nerves made her voice a little higher. "Things are going very well. Aidan has been a dream." She spoke rapidly, trying to dispel an odd ache in her chest. "He's supportive, but gives me the autonomy I like. I couldn't ask for a better managing director." She stumbled to a halt.

"Birmingham." He sounded tense.

"Excuse me?"

"We're headed to Birmingham. We have a site there and I want to show you what they do."

He launched into an explanation of the scope of Sterling International, its sites, and brief outlines of each division. "Besides," he tagged on, "you could be based in one of the satellite offices rather than London, eventually."

"Oh, but—"

"Yes?"

"I assumed I would stay in London. That's where the financial economics team is based, yes?"

"Well, don't. You could be at any one of our offices, depending on the needs of the business. Is that a problem?"

Her brow creased before smoothing back out. "No. There's no problem."

There would be a big problem if he wanted to toss her out into the countryside away from everyone else on the economics team. She was a world class professional, for God's sake.

But for now, she'd let it rest. He was trying to get a rise out of her. Something had triggered his mood and the resulting atmosphere in the small car was oppressive. Of course, it never hurt to remind him that she wouldn't be bullied. He didn't have all the leverage.

And she wasn't John Sinclair's daughter for nothing. She knew how to play games, how to play people.

"In fact, I can't remember any other companies offering me a country or smaller town setting. Sterling International certainly keeps things unique."

She smirked out the window, watching the countryside as it flew by. She'd seen the muscle bunch in his jaw, knowing she'd scored a direct hit.

Suddenly, everything was brighter again.

***

The sky streaked inky indigos with mottled purples by the time Bennett pulled his Aston Martin curbside to Devon's flat. Arrogantly double-parked, he cut the engine and turned in his seat to look her straight on. "Can I offer you dinner?" Seeing her hesitation, he added, "I kept you later than intended and I know you haven't eaten."

The words were out before he fully decided to say them. All day, she'd alternately frustrated and entranced him. In the car earlier, he'd nearly weakened. She'd been so charmingly direct, stumbling over herself when she'd basically told him how attractive he was. She'd eaten him up with those foggy gray eyes, nearly making him pull the car over to return the favor. He shifted, uncomfortable.

She interrupted his fantasies of her lush mouth and memories of their kiss with rejection. "I'd best not. But thank you."

He stared, willing his body under control. Was he wrong? Was she more interested in Aidan? She'd leapt to sing his praises earlier. He inwardly cursed himself. She was driving him insane and this was exactly what he meant to avoid. This *madness*.

What was it about this woman that made him forget every rule he'd ever made? Every lesson he'd ever learned? An image of Olivia intruded on his thoughts. Desire was abruptly and immediately vanquished.

He didn't really know Devon. He'd certainly known Olivia very well and she'd still managed to devastate him with her utter and absolute betrayal. He didn't want to be used and manipulated ever again.

With a curt nod, he said, "Then I'll see you to your door."

He was up and out of the car while she awkwardly fumbled to grab her bag, "Really, that's not…"

Holding her door open, Bennett patiently waited for her to alight. Ignoring her objections, he followed her to her apartment on the ground floor. He waited while she unlocked her flat, crowding close on the small stoop. As the lock gave, her head fell back with a quiet exhale. But Bennett was already headed down the stairs, waving a hand.

Looking back, he ordered, "Lock that door. And be early tomorrow."

He was gone before he could hear her curse.

***

Devon eyed up the sleek helicopter sitting atop Sterling International's London headquarters. She looked over at the man standing beside it, waiting for her to join him. "I had no idea this was even here."

"Well, I hardly fly it in to work every morning." Bennett smirked, patiently holding the cockpit door open.

Over the past weeks, they'd established a fragile but friendly rapport. She'd worked and traveled beside Bennett almost exclusively, learning the man and his mind. He was always demanding, and often rude. Sometimes like today, he was funny and charming.

A throaty laugh rumbled free. "No, but it's bad enough you drive an Aston Martin. Honestly, Bennett. How obvious."

He clutched his chest. "You don't like my car? That wounds me."

"I doubt your ego is even dented."

"I don't believe it. Look me in the eyes and tell me you really don't like my car."

Devon walked closer to look him dead in the eye. "I really don't like your car. It's vulgar."

Bennett staggered dramatically before recovering himself. "You lie. I've seen the secret caresses you give the armrests. The flirty glances you give my bonnet."

She burst out laughing. "Oh all right! It's a nice car."

"*Nice?* Chrysler sedans are *nice*, Devon. Aston Martins are luxury performance vehicles. We need to work on your education." He gave the door of the helicopter a light tap, nodding to her. "Now stop avoiding it and jump in."

***

Bennett helped Devon with all the unfamiliar straps before handing her the headphones. He gave the pilot a thumbs up, seeing her clutch her hands together as the rotors started to spin. The helicopter took off with a slight lurch and sharply banked into the bright sunshine over London.

He watched her, his eyes hidden behind silver rimmed aviators. They'd spent endless hours together over the past weeks, learning each other's habits and routines. He'd searched, wished for something that would lessen his fascination with her. But his desire burned, simmering under a reserved mask of gracious professionalism.

He ached, yearned for her.

The more he came to know of her, the more he wanted. She was viciously smart with a fascinating wit that never failed to disarm him. He reminded himself he didn't date staff but stopped trying to remember why.

She gasped, marveling at the panoramic view before them. Turning to him with a wide smile, she exclaimed, "Look! Isn't it magnificent?" She turned back to the windows, joyfully taking in the scene.

"Yes. Magnificent," he said hoarsely. The sun had caught the chestnut in her hair.

She swiveled, her brows raised. But he was looking out the windows, same as she had been.

***

On the roof tarmac below them, Natalie watched as Bennett and Devon flew towards the office in Leeds. They'd laughed and joked. Even though they kept a respectable distance, she'd noticed the way they leaned in and gazed at each other, especially when they thought the other wasn't looking. As Devon prepared to board the helicopter, Bennett's hand had hovered behind her back, silently protecting her in case she slipped.

Natalie closed the rooftop door, hugging herself in the sudden draft of the staircase.

She tried to recall if Bennett looked at her the way he did Devon.

Had he ever?

***

Back in London after a long day in Leeds, Bennett held out a hand to help Devon down from the helicopter. She only hesitated for a second, but it was enough to set his teeth on edge. She'd been difficult all day. Now she physically shied from him? His brows lowered as palpable tension crackled where their palms met.

She jumped down with a sigh, pulling away to head for the rooftop stairwell at a quick clip. Bennett easily caught up, despite her long-legged stride. With a grim smile, he held the door while she stepped inside, poised to flee. He made a snap decision.

"Right. How long before you're ready to step back out for some dinner?"

"Dinner?" The horror on her face might have been funny in other circumstances.

"I'm taking you to dinner. A business dinner, Devon." He sneered slightly, gratified when she visibly bristled. "Be assured that I am ready for this day to end as much as you but we still have a few things to wrap up. Now can you freshen up here or do you need to stop off at home first?"

She snapped, "Here. I'll be ready in fifteen."

"Good. I'll meet you in your office."

Bennett stalked off, perverse satisfaction curving his lips. Despite everything, he wanted more time with her. Her distant politeness and that prissy Southern tone she adopted when she was trying to hold him off ignited his baser instincts.

It was only dinner. He was in control. He would *stay* in control.

***

They were back outside on the pavement before he spoke to her again. "There's a place not far from here that's good. I own a stake in it, as a silent partner. I'd like your opinion, in fact. Are you okay with walking?"

Devon was irritable. Miles out of her depth, she'd spent all day resisting Bennett and her reserves were low. There'd been enough tension in the helicopter on the way back to London to cut it with a knife, and yet whenever she'd looked at him, he'd been as cool as ever. In the meantime, she felt hot. Bothered.

"Yes, I can walk. Why wouldn't I?"

He just looked at her, not responding to her sharp question, which only exasperated her further.

"And how do you know they have anything I want to eat? Maybe I have allergies."

He pressed a hand to her shoulder, pausing her outside a newly opened gastropub. "Stop it. You're being difficult and churlish. I expected more grace from you."

She flushed. As a southern woman, manners were important. So were apologies. "I'm sorry."

"Accepted. Now can we get on with it?"

She nodded and he silently ushered her inside. After settling into a small booth in the chic, yet intimate dining area, her stomach growled its approval. His lips curved, creasing his cheeks with humor.

"I guess we've shared enough working lunches for you to know I don't have allergies." Shamefaced, she grinned in return.

"I suppose we have. But we've never shared dinner. And never alone." He ordered a bottle of red just as the waiter stopped by to prattle off the daily specials along with recommendations for wine and beer. The pub seemed to specialize in small plates, but also served entrees.

Devon looked around, taking in the dark surroundings relieved only by the flickering warmth of candles on tables and amber sconces along the walls. It was a close atmosphere, where tables and booths crowded people together. Couples whispered while the discreet sound of sultry blues murmured in the background.

It was hardly the place for business. It was certainly not the place for her to cool off and resist the man whose knee now casually bumped her own. She narrowed her eyes on the wine as the waiter reappeared, uncorking the bottle and pouring a small amount in a glass for Bennett.

He waved him along, declining the sample, and took the bottle to pour both glasses, handing one across to her.

She took a cautious sip, finding it excellent, before sliding it just to the side. Lightly, she drummed her fingers on the table, before asking, "So, won't it be a bit difficult for us to work here? I mean, it's dark."

"Let's order food first, shall we? I'm starving."

Taking an impatient breath, she perused the menu. Normally, she loved to sample several different items, but there was no way she was sharing food and trading bites with Bennett. She'd stick to an entrée.

"If it's okay with you, I'd like to order some small plates."

Looking up from her menu, she met his level look with one of her own. "Of course." Snapping her menu closed, she said, "You pick. I like everything. Surprise me."

With an unholy gleam in his eyes, he ordered a variety of shared plates, sexy finger foods prepared with an aim to engaging all the senses in pleasure. "I love good food. My granddad taught me to cook, and I like to indulge my palate." Taking a sip of wine, he asked, "Do you like to cook, Devon?"

Dumbly, she stared. "I have no idea. I never learned."

"If you want to, let me know. I'll line you up with my grandfather. He'll teach anyone he can get his hands on." He smiled, his eyes running over her. "So your mother was no southern domestic diva?" He laughed, but she froze at the mention of her mother, causing him to stop. "Devon? What is it?"

She shook her head, forcing a smile. "Nothing. No, my mother wasn't." She stuttered to a halt. "Well, I should say that I wouldn't know if she was. She left when I was very young. And my father raised me."

Instinctively, he started to reach for her, but thankfully the food arrived. Devon breathed deeply, swallowing and fidgeting to unroll her silverware from the napkin. Taking an exaggerated interest in the server, she listened as they explained each dish. She determinedly avoided Bennett's eyes. Finally, she felt his attention ease.

Viewing the plates, she tried to spear a marinated olive with a small pick when he stopped her by laying a light hand on her wrist. "Just pick it up. Like this." Taking the olive, he popped it into her open mouth before she could protest. She felt his index finger reach inside to the soft interior of her lip before retreating. Unconsciously, she chased it with her tongue.

Bennett's lips tilted in a faint curve while his fingers briefly tightened on his wineglass. Taking a long sip, he set the glass down, seemingly relaxed.

Confused, Devon mirrored his actions and drank the earthy Italian red he'd selected to have with their dinner. A light flush warmed her cheeks, but she knew it was from her overactive response to him feeding her. Had she imagined that shared moment of temptation? Glancing over, Bennett lolled indolently against the back of the booth.

Apparently.

She popped a ham croquette into her mouth, appraising him. Her teeth broke through the crispy breading to sink into the soft creaminess of the cheese and ham interior. She moaned lightly in approval.

Bennett watched with fierce concentration. Locking his eyes on hers, he squeezed lemon on the plate of raw oysters they'd ordered. He selected one before tipping it back to slide into his mouth. Devon observed, fascinated, as the muscles in his throat moved as he swallowed.

She reached for her wine again, only to find her glass empty. She stared for a second, blank.

"Let me get that for you," Bennett neatly poured more wine for her before lightly topping off his own.

He met her eyes, his mouth tilting up on one side.

Devon cleared her throat. "I want to hear more about your grandfather. Didn't he found Sterling International?"

Bennett paused for long moment, considering. Then he surprised her by launching into a thumbnail history. Fifty-odd years ago, Charles Sterling entered the world of banking and finance as an entrepreneur with a small inheritance. He'd succeeded more wildly than anyone expected, but gladly handed over the reins first to his own son, then Bennett when

Charles II died unexpectedly and early in a car accident with his young wife. Bennett had only been in his early twenties, just out of university.

Devon clapped a hand over her mouth. "Oh God, I'm so sorry, Bennett. I didn't know. I assumed your parents were still alive, retired somewhere." At his nod of acknowledgment, she continued, "And your grandfather? Did he come back out of retirement when they passed?" At his look of confusion, she clarified, "To help you?"

"No. Nan was too distraught after losing her only child. She needed him more."

Devon wondered whom Bennett had needed. Who had been there for him?

He continued, "Then she fell ill. I always felt it was the grief, but of course that's ridiculous. Cancer was the culprit. She fought it like a warrior for three years, but eventually lost the battle. She needed Granddad. And he was there." Whenever he mentioned his grandfather, the words spoke of respect and friendship. His voice, the tone, spoke of love.

Devon leaned forward, whispering. "I don't know what to say, Bennett. You've suffered so much loss. I don't think I could stand it."

Bennett straightened, leaning forward to top off her wine again and add a splash to his. "You could. We do what we have to and we adapt. It's the human condition." He didn't drink, just idly twirled the stem of his glass. "But that's enough about me. Tell me about yourself." If he noticed her abrupt withdrawal, he ignored it. "Did you move around a bit growing up?"

In the process of reaching for her wine, Devon's hand stopped for one beat before resuming.

Eyes narrowing, Bennett continued, "Or did you stay in one place?"

She shifted in her seat. "We moved a bit. Why?"

"Sometimes you have more of an accent than others. I guessed that's because you didn't consistently live all your life in the South. Am I right?"

She chuckled, carefully not meeting his eyes. "Well, that depends on what you define as the South. And that depends on where you are in the States. It's all relative, you see." She swirled her wine, but also didn't sip. "Did it bother you being an only child?"

"No. I attended boarding schools so had lots of mates. I never really thought about it, to be honest. Then my parents died and it was all far too late."

Devon cringed. She wanted to shift the conversation away from herself, but she'd been thoughtless. Guilt flushing her cheeks, she reached across the table, forgetting her vow not to touch.

"I'm sorry, that was insensitive."

He squeezed her fingers before quickly releasing them. She had one moment to miss the contact before he questioned her again.

"So tell me more about your family."

His midnight gaze was intent. Picking up her dinner napkin, she began to restlessly pleat it between her fingers. "Why?"

"Because we're enjoying some friendly after-dinner chat." His voice hardened. "Like civilized people do, Devon."

She twisted the pleats into a tight spiral. She had little doubt how uncivilized Bennett Sterling would be if he had any idea about *her* family. Who she came from. What she was. "I think we should get to work. That's what we came here to do, didn't we?" Seeing his brows lower, she pushed further. "Didn't we?"

Bennett's eyes narrowed. He spread his hand on the table between them and grated, "I'm getting tired of your disrespect. And I'm wondering why you can't answer a simple question about your family."

Devon paled, but knew she mustn't weaken. She had everything to lose if she revealed too much to his probing. He'd fire her in a heartbeat if he knew her father was a practiced grifter, adept at confidence games.

As was she.

It only proved what she'd known all along. He was not for her, could never be for someone like her. They were worlds apart.

There was no common ground between them. He would never, ever understand. Even now, she could see the distrust clouding his eyes. Already, he sneered with disbelief and was opening his mouth to continue.

She needed to stop this. Now. "No, you're being disrespectful. You're prying into my personal business when I'm clearly uncomfortable talking to you." She watched as he rocked back with a quick shake of his head. A dull flush darkened his cheeks. She pressed on, ruthlessly driving her point. "You have to admit this is hardly a business dinner! There hasn't been one speck—"

"Enough." He smacked his palm down on the wood, alarming her. Several patrons looked their way. "*Enough*," he hissed again before signaling for the tab and paying in angry silence. Grabbing her wrist, he marched her outside of the restaurant.

By this point, her shock wore off and she was smoldering. "Let go of me!"

Throwing her wrist away from him, he stalked away for a few paces before spinning back.

Devon took the opportunity to trudge off in the opposite direction, uncaring whether he followed. He quickly caught up, breathing deeply. She immediately laid into him.

"I can make my own way home. I don't want you with me."

She was confused when he huffed out a laugh, mumbling something about her *prissy voice*. She should ignore him. The man was clearly insane.

She increased her pace, further aggravated when he managed to easily accommodate her stride. She risked a glance and found him glaring back at her.

She stopped walking, disconcerted by his overt anger. "Would you please go away? I need a break from you. And it's pretty clear you need a break from me."

He jerked to a halt. He started to reach for her shoulders, but then let his hands drop. "Devon, I'm not going to leave you to walk home alone. This is non-negotiable. I have reached the end of my rope with you, so I'm going to have to politely ask you to *shut up and deal with it*." As she opened her mouth to protest, he raised a finger to stop her. She closed her mouth. "The sooner we get walking, the sooner you get home. Can we get on with it?"

She said nothing, simply resumed walking at a furious pace. As usual, he caught up with her in moments. When his arm casually brushed hers, she shot him a deadly glare.

"Would it help if I stay on my side of the imaginary line?"

"You know, Bennett, I have two perfectly good shoes that would love to make your acquaintance."

He snorted but she nearly laughed aloud when she caught him risking a glance toward her feet. Lucky for him, she'd chosen simple flats that day.

Hardly worth the effort.

CHAPTER SIX

DEVON STRODE INTO HER OFFICE at Sterling International an hour before her usual time. She felt uncomfortable, uncertain where she stood after last night's debacle with Bennett. And Devon wasn't used to feeling unsure. So, she fell back on things that came naturally and automatically.

Intellect. Performance. Excellence.

She wouldn't let him continue to charm her into blurring the boundaries between them. She'd relaxed her guard. And it wasn't as though she were a stranger to charisma. She certainly had her own fair share and used it to effect while growing up when the situation demanded.

Besides, it wasn't as though anything profoundly personal had happened since their kiss.

And that was a relief, she convinced herself. She couldn't fight the attraction he held for her. She ignored the slight ache in her stomach at the thought of him as she punched the elevator for the twentieth floor.

I must stop wanting Bennett Sterling. He could never accept my family, my background.

I can never have Bennett Sterling.

As she counted the floors going up, she repeated it to herself. The previous evening had been a timely and blunt reminder. If she'd felt stimulated and excited, it was only because he was so adept at seducing women. And she wasn't used to spending time with such dynamic and attractive men. Not personal time anyway, thinking of the male colleagues she had blissfully ignored up to this point. *And Dom doesn't count either.*

But when she'd resisted his attempts to dig into her personal life, she'd glimpsed Bennett's real opinion of her. And it wasn't something she wanted. She couldn't afford his attention or interest. It would only lead to distrust and anger, just the way last night had.

I can never have Bennett Sterling.

The elevator doors opened to find the subject of her thoughts sitting on the corner of Natalie's desk outside his office. They spoke too softly for her to catch what was being said. But the familiarity she'd sensed from the first time she'd seen them together was back in force. Hearing the doors swish open, two sets of blue eyes swung toward her.

Her voice pitched higher than usual, Devon greeted them. "Good morning. You're both early."

Bennett remained seated, but straightened so he faced her. "Yes, we wanted to leave promptly for Manchester today. How are you this morning?"

His eyes searched hers, but Devon looked down in avoidance. "I'm good, glad I'm here then." She waved a hand towards the hall. "I'll drop my things so we can be off." She frowned, seeing Natalie's tiny smirk.

Bennett spoke, drawing the attention of both women. "Natalie, would you please mind getting us some coffee? I'd like to have a private word with Devon." He waited for his PA to walk away before continuing, "Devon, you won't be going as I no longer require your presence. Natalie will accompany me and you can remain here and catch up on your other projects."

She blanched, feeling the lash of his professionalism. He sounded stilted, not at all like the man she'd grown used to over the past weeks. With an aching tightness in her throat, she swallowed. Blinking rapidly, she desperately tried to rally her earlier thoughts.

I can never have Bennett Sterling.

Natalie returned, coffees in hand. Turning to Devon, she said, "I never asked, but I hope you like it strong. Personally, I have no taste for anything weak."

Devon met her sharp stare. Thankful for the reminder, she straightened to her full height, taking the coffee. "I'm sure it's perfect. I'll wish you both bon voyage as I have work to do. Good day."

She walked away, steel in her spine. She never looked back even though she felt Bennett's gaze boring into her.

He was not for her.

***

"Where the hell is she?" Bennett paced in front of Natalie's desk, having waited for Devon to return to her office for the last fifteen minutes.

Natalie looked up through her lashes. "I don't know. I didn't know ten minutes ago. I still don't."

He stopped. Tucking his hands in his pockets, he leaned over her. "Make an effort, dammit. Find her." Turning on his heel, he went into his office, slamming the door behind him.

Weeks had passed since he'd stopped traveling and working so closely with Devon. And he missed her, unbearably. He'd found himself in her office on some semblance of catching up over coffee when she failed to appear. He panicked, worried she'd left the business again.

Natalie breezed into his office. "She's stepped out for a bit with Aidan. They've been working together on projects, and she's been downstairs quite a lot, apparently. They expect them to be back soon."

Turning, she walked back to the door. Over her shoulder, she tossed, "Is there anything else?"

"Call a meeting. Ten minutes with me, Aidan and Devon. Boardroom."

Natalie stopped to look at him fully. "And how are they supposed to know about this meeting if they're not here?"

Bennett eyed her steadily. "They have phones. They should be checking them." He waited until she'd reached the door before continuing. "Oh and Natalie?"

"Yes?"

"Don't forget about the gallery tonight. I'll pick you up by six." She brightened at his reminder. "Let's go out for a drink after. I need to talk to you."

She nodded, her smile fading a little.

Bennett waited until she was gone before spinning his chair to look out across the London skyline to the dome of St. Paul's Cathedral. He'd bought tickets for this evening's art exhibition months ago as a gift to her. He could see no point in canceling now, but would use the evening for a long overdue discussion.

He hadn't missed the churlish looks Natalie had been giving Devon since she arrived months ago. He was certain Devon had picked up on her behavior and jumped to all kinds of wrong conclusions for it.

He hadn't decided yet what he wanted from Devon, what he wanted them to be. But he knew Natalie and what he *didn't* want with her. It was past time he made sure she knew too.

***

Meanwhile, on a break cheated from work, Devon ran through the wrought iron gates of St. Dunstan in the East to immediately stop in wonder. The entrance opened onto a stately tower, tall and gothic, mildewed by time. The steeple looked deceptively fragile, but she knew from her research it was strong. It had survived the fires both man and nature launched. She grinned at the man beside her.

"We'll have to practically run through it so we're not gone too long." Grabbing Aidan's hand, she set off, laughing into the cloudless bright blue of the autumn sky.

All around, working professionals from the City of London were milling about, either sitting on benches or casually walking through the park. Some were grabbing a quick coffee or snack while others spoke to colleagues in hushed tones, likely discussing whatever was keeping them busy that day.

The grounds of the park at St. Dunstan included an old church that had stood on the property since 1100 AD. Over the centuries, it gained additions, and then lost them, when fire or attacking enemies decided to raze its sacred halls. The proud tower, added over three hundred years ago by Sir Christopher Wren, still commanded a piece of the busy financial district's skyline. She was grateful for it.

Rounding a corner, they emerged onto ruins that were overgrown with creeping vines and lush greenery. Devon stopped, letting the hushed stillness fill her.

She squeezed Aidan's hand, prompting him to listen with her. "Shh. So we can hear."

He paused, looking around the park with puzzled eyes. "What do you hear, Devon?"

"Peace. Hundreds, thousands of souls have walked here before us. They whisper in the leaves, sigh on the wind. And yet it's so peaceful, Aidan." Letting her gaze swing around the scene back to the man beside her, she said, "I'm sorry. I get imaginative in old places." She laughed a little. "You should see me in cemeteries, I'm practically fanciful."

"No, you sounded sad. Are you?"

Sighing, she looked around once more, wistful eyes lingering on the haunting wildness around her. Frowning, she said, "I'm not. This reminds me a little of Savannah, Georgia, back in the States. It's a special place to me. I spent time there growing up. It's not nearly as old, but there's a timelessness to both that draws me in." She looked back at Aidan with earnest eyes. "People don't stay, but I guess I'm comforted by the buildings and places that do."

His eyebrows drew together. "Devon, some people *do* stay, you know."

"Of course. I didn't mean to suggest they didn't." She spoke quickly, changing the subject. She didn't look at him, but at her watch instead. "We should get back. Even though it's Friday afternoon, we don't want to be missed. But thank you so much for bringing me." She risked a glance and decided she didn't care for the pained concern staring back at her from Aidan's eyes. "Does Jane like it here?"

Jane was Aidan's girlfriend of more than two years. Devon met her on a recent weekend where the three of them had accidentally run into each other at an art fair in Hyde Park. The two women hit it off right away and Devon considered her a fast friend. Aidan was crazy for Jane and never missed an opportunity to talk about her.

"She does," he exclaimed. "We meet here for lunch sometimes and she always enjoys it. Janie has a taste for the spirit of a place, like you." They were walking fast and had reached the gates again by the time he finished talking.

"See, Aidan? That's why I like her. Jane and I are kindred spirits. Which is all the more reason for you to marry her." She poked him in the ribs, impishly prodding him while uttering the joke she'd been repeating after meeting his girlfriend. Since befriending Aidan, she revealed more of herself than usual. No longer just the serious young woman from months ago, she easily slipped into the role of mischievous matchmaker.

He smiled. "If you must know, I *am* asking her to marry me." Devon stopped walking for a second, unaccountably pleased. He continued, "This weekend. So stop harassing me and wish me luck instead."

Swamping him in a spontaneous hug, Devon wished him the best and assured him he had nothing to worry about. "She's nuts for you. And I don't know of two people more perfect for each other."

"Thank you," he said while flushing a little. "Maybe we can convince you that some people do stick."

***

"Next time we go out, I'll take you to Bunhill Fields Burial Ground. Since you have a thing for cemeteries, you'll love that place. It's free too, and right here in the City of London, so you're squaring up to be a perfect date." Aidan tossed Devon a bottled water as he teased her while lounging on the corner of her desk. Both of them were still flushed from hurrying back from St. Dunstan. She laughed, uncapping the bottle to take a long drink.

Neither saw the brooding man in the doorway watching both of them with dark intensity.

"Next time you *go out*, I'll thank you to be back in time for scheduled meetings." Bennett spoke harshly, startling them both. "In fact, Aidan, I'm not sure you should be *going out* with fellow staffers at all. Aren't you engaged? Jane, isn't it?"

Devon interjected, trying to help. "Actually he's not." She fumbled, "I mean, he's about to be, but he isn't. Yet. Well…" She stopped, swallowing nervously.

Aidan spoke up. "I'm sorry, but what scheduled meeting?"

Bennett swung his glare back to the other man. "You're both late for a meeting I called in the boardroom. I expect you to check your messages, even when you're out." His gaze raked them both, top to bottom. "Of course, I hardly thought you'd be out taking postage stamp tours on company time." He turned on his heel, pulling open Devon's door. "Now both of you, get your things together and meet me in five. *As requested.*"

By the time Bennett was in the elevator, his jaw ached from grinding his teeth together. Planting his feet wide, he stabbed the button for the correct floor and took several deep breaths.

He was being an overbearing, pompous ass.

But seeing Devon happy with another man had thrown him. He hadn't expected the sudden constriction of his lungs, the inability to breathe when he'd seen her laughing with Aidan. Possessiveness, swift and primal, erupted within him. The asinine notions he'd harbored for resisting her faded.

Was his grandfather right? Was he essentially punishing Devon for something Olivia did so long ago?

Bennett exited the elevator with unusual restlessness. He had a lot to think about, but this wasn't the time. Aidan and Devon looked up expectantly as he entered the boardroom. They quickly looked back down again, murmuring over the shared data they viewed on their laptops. They sat close, huddled so they could better see each other's screens.

Instantly, his mood soured further. He felt excluded. Isolated.

"Devon," he barked, impatient with her lack of attention to him.

"Yes?" She patiently answered, not rising to his provocation.

"Update me on steel hedges. Concisely." He deliberately asked for something she hadn't worked on. The devil rode him, wanting her to feel a fraction of his discomfort, the unrelenting uncertainty that plagued him when she was near.

She looked helplessly at Aidan, lost. "I apologi—"

Aidan fielded the question, only adding to Bennett's frustration. They worked fluidly as a team now, aided by weeks of seamless integration when Bennett had tossed them together while he flew off to the sites with Natalie.

He clenched his fist before smoothing it back out on the table before him. "That's very good, Aidan." He trained his gaze on Devon. "Devon, you're relying on Aidan to answer your questions. That's not nearly good enough, especially for me." Her gasp of outrage caused one side of his mouth to lift in triumph. "A little less time sightseeing and a little more time working, hmm?"

He made sure he was out the door before she could think of a reply. Or worse.

***

Devon fumed, rapidly laying the final touches on reports she and Aidan had worked on for weeks. Taking a final look before approving it, she printed out a copy and marched down the hallway to Bennett's door. With a token raise of her brows to Natalie, she walked right in, crossing the room's wide expanse to arrive at his desk. He was swiveled away, apparently deep in thought as he stared out the window to his impressive view.

She smacked the report down on his desk and took a seat, waiting.

Bennett pushed a foot to swing his chair around to face her.

She flicked a casual hand toward the report. "It's the hedge fund project. Global top twenty with Euro, Asian, and North American region subsets. Top ten funds outlined with projected earnings along with potential vulnerabilities." She rose to full height, staring him down. "This is what I was assigned, not just commodities or steel. And it's a full week early. I worked hard on this."

She was heading for the door before he spoke. "Devon."

She stopped, freezing in place.

"Get back here."

She went back to the chair she'd vacated and took a seat. He never looked at her, just continued to read the report she'd given him. After a few minutes, he looked up, running his hand over the faint stubble on his jaw.

"It's good. I have to take a longer look, but you did a good job." He continued to eye her levelly. "And way before schedule."

She moved to rise, feeling validated but still angry with him. "May I go?"

She thought she heard him sigh.

"Yes." He hesitated before adding, "I'm sorry. You probably haven't had a chance to see much of London or the UK." He ran two fingers inside the collar of his shirt, as if loosening it. "Perhaps I could serve as tour guide sometime. I did grow up here, after all."

She stopped in the act of getting up to gape at him. Pressing a hand to the fluttery feeling in her stomach, she involuntarily glanced over her shoulder to the exit. Bennett cleared his throat, bringing her attention back to him.

"Forget it. Obviously, it's such a big decision for you," he said gruffly. "Christ, it's not like I proposed."

Once again, the man could fling her from one mood to the next with lightning speed. As spots of color reddened her cheeks, she pursed her lips, trying to hold herself back.

It was no use. He was *maddening.*

"We both know that's never happening, as you've made it so clear in the past," she said loudly. His eyes widened on hers. "It's best I stay away from you, though, for my own good. *I don't want to get any ideas above my station.*"

She thought she heard him curse as she slammed out his door.

***

The art exhibition was in full swing when Devon entered the Courtauld Gallery later that evening. She

96

was no stranger to attending events alone, and most times she'd have said she preferred to view art without the distraction of someone else's nattering. But she was feeling lonely tonight, sick of her own company. Idly, she wished Dominic were here. He'd pushed his visit back a couple of times already. Now he was vague about his arrival. She wondered if he'd come at all now, considering his schedule and how busy he was.

She sighed. It really wasn't Dominic she wanted beside her anyway. She missed Bennett. Even when he enraged her, she was more stimulated and enervated than she'd ever been with anyone else in her life. He drew her in, entrancing her with his many facets.

She toured the displayed artwork, oblivious to the admiring glances being cast her way. She wore unrelenting black, to suit her mood and the setting. A cowled sweater dress was cinched by a leather hip belt and finished with plain-heeled boots. Silver hoops shone at her ears where her dark hair had been pulled back into a messy chignon.

She stopped to view a magnificent wall mural when a deep voice spoke behind her. "Hello Devon. Fancy meeting you here."

Her heart beat once, then again before she looked behind her to see Bennett and Natalie, standing close. He had changed from earlier, but still managed to look expensive and virile in vintage denims with a black roll neck sweater. Where he was dark, Natalie was light. She wore cream slacks paired with a while silk blouse that complemented her pale blonde beauty and created a striking contrast to Bennett's dangerous attraction.

Devon hugged herself, false bravado masking the thickness clogging her throat. "Well. Who knew London could be so small?" She avoided Bennett's eyes by smiling widely at Natalie. "I'll leave you to tour the exhibit. Have a nice evening."

Bennett started to interrupt, but Natalie hooked her arm through his. She said, "Yes, Bennett. Why don't we leave Devon be? She probably sees enough of us at work as it is."

Devon continued smiling, blinded by the moisture beginning to fill her eyes. She abruptly turned, wanting and needing to get away. She blinked rapidly, absently walking back the way she'd come. As she rounded a corner into the foyer, she looked back at Bennett and Natalie.

They seemed to be murmuring quietly to each other, Bennett stooping to hear what the other woman said. An intense longing struck Devon, causing an ache near her heart. She pressed her palm to it, closing her eyes against the sight of the couple until it finally eased.

Quietly, she set her glass of wine down on a nearby table and left.

***

"Dirty martini, vodka, please."

Devon placed her order and sank onto one of the high padded leather seats that lined the bar in the pub she and Bennett had visited weeks before. She refused to examine why she chose it, especially knowing Bennett was an owner.

So much had happened since their last visit here, they were scarcely the same people. Then, they'd shared bites after a companionable day's work. Now, she barely saw him when he wasn't traveling with Natalie to one of his sites or closeted in meetings. Natalie was with him in those too, usually perched near his right elbow typing minutes or providing details before he could ask for them. Devon told herself that was normal; she was his PA.

But when Devon saw Bennett, he barely spoke to her. In fact, most communications now came through Natalie.

Natalie, Natalie, Natalie.

Tonight, he'd been out with her on a date. Clearly, his employee dating embargo didn't extend to *Natalie.*

Devon took a long sip of her martini, savoring the icy vodka before it smoothed down the tightness of her throat. Seeing Bennett and Natalie wrapped arm in arm had been unexpected. Pain and jealousy ambushed her before she could brace herself. The entire evening and, if she were honest, the weeks leading up to it, had taken their toll.

She hurt.

She had a feeling she might get a little drunk. She caught the eye of the bartender to move that plan forward. "I'll have another."

He prepared it with maximum efficiency and minimal flourish. He presented it, saying, "This one's taken care of." When she started to protest, he added, "Couple over there."

Devon craned her neck to see where he pointed. In a far corner away from her, sharing a small booth, were Bennett and Natalie. They were seated side by side, sharing the same bench.

Unbelievable.

She caught Bennett's eye, and raised her glass in a mocking toast. Natalie merely cracked a smile before taking a sip of her white wine.

Devon downed her martini in one very long swallow. Setting it back down on the bar, she met the bartender's level look. Without words, he set to making another.

"Make it extra dirty, please."

He added the extra juice before tossing a few additional olives in as well. "This one's on me. You have style. *And* stamina. I like that."

She sipped the new martini with slightly more caution, trying to ignore the pain ripping through her. "Well, we're about to find out about the stamina. Watch this space."

***

Bennett tried, he really did. He watched as Devon finished a third martini before polishing off a fourth. She carefully rose from her stool before heading for the restroom. She resolutely avoided looking toward the table he and Natalie shared. His eyes bored into her as she approached, determined that she acknowledge him.

Of course, she didn't.

He'd passed this evening in the company of a beautiful woman, albeit his PA. They'd viewed exquisite art and drank superior wine. Yet, he couldn't care less. In fact, he'd been forced to have one of the most painfully awkward conversations of his adult life sitting in this booth with Natalie. In doing so, he knew he'd hurt her. When she'd teared up, he'd shifted to share the bench with her, to hold her hand. He'd never meant for her to get the wrong idea about them. But she had, and now he'd had to set her straight.

He shifted, heaving a deep breath before taking a drink of his wine. He scowled into the glass before setting it back on the table. To add to his aggravations, all he wanted was a damn martini.

Devon was driving him out of his mind. She seemed so wounded and lost in the gallery. When he looked for her, she'd disappeared. Gone. Now she was here, the worst place she could be when he was having his all-important talk with Natalie.

Devon distracted him. Provoked him.

She sat at that bar, drinking martinis, uncaring. Probably flirting with the bartender.

She enticed him. Attracted him.

She stopped near their table on her return trip, minutely swaying on her feet. "Enjoying yourselves?" She owlishly eyed both Bennett and Natalie, squinting at the distance between them.

Abruptly, he realized she was a little, if not a lot, drunk.

He unconsciously scooted over, to put some space between himself and Natalie. He stopped when Natalie turned her head to glare, chin held high. A flush warmed his face and he thanked the darkness of the bar's interior.

Devon, damn her, watched the interchange with belligerent sass. With hand on hip, brow cocked, she openly stared until even Natalie began to fidget. "You two seem to be having a good time. It's cozy in here, isn't it?" She didn't wait for an answer, just winked insouciantly. But not before he'd seen something flash into her eyes, briefly darkening them before it was gone.

Was she distressed? Hurt?

She walked stiffly back to her seat, as though her knees weren't bending quite properly. As she settled back in, the bartender reappeared, questioning her pallor.

"What's gone wrong? What's happened to you?"

Before Devon could answer, Bennett's deep voice interrupted. "As much as I hate to interfere with another man's play, I really think this one's had enough to drink."

"Now wait a minute, mate—"

"No, you wait." Bennett's level stare had the bartender backing up a step. He hitched a thumb in the direction of his booth. "I sat right there and watched.

You may not have realized it, but you over served her. Now, I'm stepping in."

Devon cleared her throat. "If you two don't mind, I'd like to speak for myself. And I'd also like another martini." She pushed her glass toward the bartender while staring at Bennett in defiance. She turned, missing his reluctant nod of assent to the bartender to begin mixing her another drink.

She carefully enunciated her words. "I resent your attitude." Bennett bit back a smile. The prissy tone she liked to adopt was starting to grow on him, especially when it was coupled with ill-concealed intoxication.

"And why are you over here anyway?" She gestured to the booth he'd left. "Natalie looks awfully lonely. And cold. Maybe you should go back and practically sit on her again. That should warm her up."

"I'll worry about Natalie." Bennett smothered a laugh. Devon was virtually green with jealousy. His mood was improving by the minute.

Devon turned her back on him. "Good. I'll just worry about my martini then. Good night."

Bennett stared at Devon's back, debating what to do. He couldn't leave her here; she was too drunk for her own good. But Natalie sat in the booth where he'd left her, drumming her fingers.

He held up a finger, signaling the bartender he'd be right back. Then he heard her.

"And good riddance."

Grasping her upper arm, he swiveled her seat around.

"What did you say?" He roared the question, his patience evaporating at her obvious desire to see him gone.

"I said, *good riddance*," she cried. "I liked this place, I thought it was special. And you brought *her* here." Devon clapped a hand over her mouth, horrified embarrassment making her eyes glow pearly gray.

Bennett was thrilled with what four and a half vodka martinis made her reveal. But as his lips started to tilt into a satisfied smile, she grabbed her drink and knocked it back, never pausing for breath. Then she fisted a hand and brought it slicing down to break his hold on her. Before he could react, she pivoted off her chair, grabbed her purse and flew out of the pub.

CHAPTER SEVEN

DEVON BREATHLESSLY RAN UP THE few stairs to her front door, desperate to beat the man hard on her heels. Cursing, she briefly fumbled her keys but it was enough to give Bennett those last needed moments to catch up to her. He wedged his foot in the door just as she slammed it, hard, on the booted leather.

"Dammit, you let me in right now, Devon. Or so help me God, I'll push this door in and you with it." He snarled the words into the gap, his voice throbbing with anger and intent.

"If you don't move your foot, I'm going to break the damn thing. Now get out!" She wasn't about to be bullied by the seething mass of angry male on the other side of her door. Giving an inch to someone like Bennett Sterling could only result in him taking a mile.

The thought was no sooner formed when he set his shoulder against the solid wood and heaved the door wide open. Although Devon staggered back two steps from his momentum, she quickly recovered.

Standing tall and angry despite his dark intimidation, she shouted, "You have one minute to get out of my house or I start yelling for help."

Bennett took one deliberate step closer, brows lowered in threat.

"I mean it. One minute!"

Another step and he was so close she could breathe his woodsy cologne. He growled into her ear, "You wouldn't *dare*. Now you're going to shut up and listen for once."

Devon allowed herself one heartbeat to indulge in the midnight abyss of his eyes. He stilled, taking her compliance for granted while she moved a deliberate step backward.

With no break in eye contact, she opened her mouth and released a blood-curdling scream.

***

Aghast, Bennett grabbed a hank of hair at her nape, jerking her to press a bruising kiss on her parted lips. He held her captured, punishing the tender flesh before invading her mouth to further taste and plunder.

He lost control. He held her still, hair fisted while his other hand slid around her waist and flattened onto her low back, arching her into his demanding bulk. As his tongue touched hers, he tasted olives and something uniquely Devon. He eased back slightly, realizing she stood immobile, barely breathing.

He was behaving like a maniac.

He breathed deep, taking a moment to claw back his sanity and some sense of himself. This was not who he was. He did not push in doors and grab women. He thought back to their beginning. Ever since his eyes had touched hers, he'd been struggling in a morass of compulsions. He wanted as never before. A hunger burned in him, but not to frighten. Never to intimidate. His heart skipped.

Her hands were trapped between them, so he flattened one of her palms against his chest, letting her feel the thunder of his heartbeat. While she kept her hand where he'd placed it, he felt the other lightly cross over his shoulder and glide down his back. Unconsciously, she soothed him. Reckless temper melted away with the stroke of her hand. And in its place was need.

He waited. When she met his gaze again, he lowered his mouth back to hers. This time, his tongue softly explored, a gentle contrast to his hard strength surrounding her. He softened his hold, pulling back slightly, whispering his lips over hers in a request, a question. He brushed his lips over her cheeks and forehead, patient.

Devon sighed her acceptance, leaning into him. He briefly kissed each of her closed eyelids before coming back to her mouth with lips that firmed again, but with desire now rather than anger.

She yielded. Opening her mouth to his searching kiss, she met his tongue while her hands came up to clasp his shoulders before settling on his muscled biceps.

"Put your arms around my neck." Bennett rasped the words into her ear.

As she obeyed, he neatly circled one arm beneath her knees and scooped her into his arms. She breathlessly tossed her head back to laugh, surprising him, while he carried her to the nearby living room.

"Honestly, I know I should protest, but I'm enjoying this too much. I could get used to this kind of treatment." Still laughing, she met his eyes just as he dropped his mouth to hers for a briefly devastating foray.

"I'll keep that in mind. You're a long, tall one, but pretty lightweight. I could carry you around half of London, but I think I'll sit instead." Cradling her on his lap, he ran one hand down the length of her legs that lay stretched out beside him. "Now, where were we?" Fitting his mouth back to hers, he proceeded to muffle any answer she might have given.

He reclined beside her, face to face. Small gasps and moans escaped while they caressed, tested, and learned each other. Tangled tongues mimicked the slide and push of a much more intimate act. Bennett unbuttoned Devon's blouse while pulling it free of her skirt. He pressed an open-mouthed kiss over one cotton-covered breast as she fumbled with his shirt buttons. She stopped, arching up and gasping with pleasure.

"My God, you're responsive. And as much as I have a new respect for American cotton, let's see with this off." Expertly, Bennett flipped open the front clasp to her bra with one hand and spread the sides apart.

Seeing a rosy blush suffuse her cheeks, Bennett shifted back to gaze at her. Refusing to meet his eyes, she diverted his hand back to her breast from where he'd raised it to touch her face. He noted her shyness, her sudden preoccupation with looking anywhere but at him.

Deciding to let it pass, he enjoyed the perfect moment of seeing her near naked for the first time. Thumbing the erect nipple of one breast, he lowered his head to blow gently over the other. Hearing her gasp, he smiled briefly against the bud before closing his mouth tightly over it and rhythmically sucking as she arched sharply against him.

Devon curved beneath him while pivoting so Bennett's weight shifted above her. He rucked up her skirt and caressed her thigh while pushing the fabric as high as it might go. Meanwhile, having finally undone the buttons on his shirt, she touched his naked skin.

She explored his chest in broad strokes before reaching over his shoulders to push his shirt over and off. Pulling him to her, she breathed, "Kiss me, Bennett." She tugged him down further.

Careful to support his weight, Bennett moved back up to her mouth and lost himself again, exploring and retreating as their tongues danced in a carnal rhythm. He should slow this down. She was innocent, he was sure. Her blushes and reactions to his touch had given her away. They were going too far, too fast. But she was so beautiful, and so willing. Reason was abandoned under the drumbeat of desire.

Just a little longer.

***

Devon took the kiss deeper, inviting his tongue into a dark duel while she pressed her pelvis into his, trying to find relief from the ache he'd aroused. There were no pretenses between them now, only giving and receiving, each generously trying to please the other.

She shifted her lower body, sinking further into the couch while his erection simultaneously notched into the softness between her legs. Her skirt bunched up, revealing dainty white panties.

Sweating, Bennett levered himself up slightly, grinning while he ogled her. "More cotton, I see. I love the little daisies."

Devon felt herself blushing furiously, unused to a man's teasing. Personally, she found distraction to be the better part of valor. In that spirit, she parted her thighs, drawing them up to hug his hips and allowing him to press further into her.

She only struggled with his belt for a moment before it released and she started work on his pants.

Satisfaction darkened her eyes as she heard him suck in an involuntary breath when she brushed his rigid shaft.

He took hold of her hands, loosely pinning them over her head. "We need to slow down."

Unfazed, Devon dragged her mouth to taste the salty skin of his neck, smiling against him when she heard his deep groan. She nipped the corded muscles there before using the flat of her tongue to quickly bathe the small bite. Sensing him strain against her, she shifted again to explore the intricate whorls of his ear while allowing the hard buds of her nipples to graze the hair of his chest.

The soft friction tore another groan from Bennett before he abruptly loosed her hands to crush her against him. She felt the pounding urgency of his heart, banging in desperate need. Sweeping her palm along his abdominals, Devon felt the strong muscles ripple in reaction. Triumphant at his response to her, she trailed her fingers to his waistband before slipping down to cup his length.

Large masculine hands gripped her thighs, pushing them further apart and up along his waist. Devon squeezed him, overcome with pleasure and desire. She felt free, unencumbered by her past. There was only this moment. And it was only she and Bennett.

Her gaze locked with his, unknowingly innocent. For once, she left herself unguarded and exposed.

Bennett stared back, his features oddly fierce before he took her mouth in a hard kiss, stealing her breath with sudden intensity. She returned his kiss, but hesitated, momentarily surprised by his raw male hunger. She slipped her hands behind his neck and stroked them down his back, unconsciously gentling him as before in one long stroke.

He stilled. Then he copied her caress by running his hands along the length of her thighs, where she had tensed in silent confusion. He smoothed his fingers over the fine cotton covering her core, quickly moving away to tease the delicate lace edges when she froze. Startled, she locked eyes with him, knowing his had never left her face.

He leaned down and grazed her lips in a soft kiss. "Please."

Devon nodded, then felt his hand slip inside her panties to cup her. One long finger slowly rubbed up and down, then returned to circle the hidden nub that throbbed in painful pleasure. Closing her eyes, she let her head fall back, sensual bliss overtaking her.

She parted her lips as Bennett lightly outlined her mouth with his tongue. When he paired the movement by slipping a finger inside her, she sharply arched her back, dragging her breasts along his torso and grinding her pelvis into him. He thrust his finger back and forth before adding a second, and rubbed the heel of his palm against her while he stroked.

Locking her ankles around him, she gasped while clutching his shoulders and rocking into him.

Eyes opening wide, she looked to him in silent entreaty.

Bennett pivoted to his shoulder to tear the filmy cotton panties away from her. He pulled her further down into the couch, which caused her skirt to bunch up completely, leaving her legs unencumbered. Abruptly, he reared back, and before she realized what he was doing, both legs were hooked over his shoulders and he lowered his head down her body.

"No." He stilled. Breathlessly, she said, "Please."

He stared hard at her, and she felt the heat in her face spreading to her neck and chest. She twitched beneath him, uncomfortable with his prolonged scrutiny. As she started to shift her leg, Bennett licked one erect nipple, and then bit it. Shocked, she bucked and peered down into devastating navy. Then he turned his attention back to her breast and suckled hard, causing her to dig her fingernails deep into his shoulders as she fought to hold herself steady. He eased off only to give attention to the other breast. Just when she thought she'd die with pleasure, his fingers were inside her again, thrusting in time with the sucking rhythm of his mouth.

There was no build up, just an abrupt shattering that caused a high cry to break from her lips before she was cut off with the bruising pressure of his mouth. The pulsing contractions continued as she pressed up into him, desperately seeking his solid strength to ground her. Devon felt close, connected to him. Her normally busy mind blanked except for the profound link she felt weaving between them.

As she came back down, and her breathing returned to something closer to normal, she felt Bennett's erection pressing into her. She reached down, cupping his girth before roughly chafing his length through his pants. He reared up, gripping her hand with steely strength to stop her.

"I'm too close."

"Then let me help." She smiled, so sure of this moment. Of him. "I want you. *All* of you, Bennett."

He gentled his hold, but kept her hand in his while he sat up on the sofa. Turning, he looked first at her face, then down her body, and back to her eyes. Embarrassed, Devon shifted but Bennett clasped her wrist before bringing it to his lips for a soft kiss on the underside.

With fingers that barely touched her skin, he rearranged her blouse to button it and helped pull her skirt back into place. Confused, Devon could only stare as he adjusted his own clothing before sitting back down next to her. He stared down at the floor, his knees spread with hands loosely clasped between them. Taking a deep breath, he turned his head to look back at her, a faint line creased between his brows.

She abruptly focused. Hastily, she straightened and stared ahead, letting the full import of the past moments soak in.

He'd withdrawn. He didn't want her.

And she had fallen at his feet. She shuddered, realizing how close she'd come to full intimacy with him. He'd tried to let her down gently. But she'd capped it all by practically begging him to sleep with her.

This could simply not be any worse.

What had happened to keeping him at a distance? Keeping him as far away from her, her father, and her past as possible?

The thought of John Sinclair steeled her spine. He'd taught her control and discipline, and she was never more grateful for it than in this moment. Ruthlessly, she summoned up her mantra from weeks ago.

I can never have Bennett Sterling.

She would repeat that as many times necessary to pound it into her thick skull. But right now, she needed to get Bennett out of her house. Again, she drew the needed strength and skills from her father. Although she'd turned her back on his world of games and grifts, preferring academia, she wasn't opposed to a little manipulation when it was necessary.

It was necessary.

"Well. This is awkward." Summoning a smile, she said, "I think this is when the British would think it's proper to offer tea. I hope you don't mind if I don't?"

Standing, she took a couple of steps to the doorway, hoping he would take the hint. She desperately ignored the fact that her panties and bra were lying somewhere out of reach, likely in pieces. Although mortified, she was determined to brazen out this horrific farce to the bitter end.

"Actually, I do mind. Tea would be wonderful. Let me help."

***

He handily reached over her to hold open the door to her galley kitchen as she preceded him. Bennett watched as she assembled the cups, saucers, and teapot for the tray, her hands moving in jerks. As she slammed the kettle on the stove, he was sure he heard a mumbled curse.

Bennett stuck his head in the refrigerator to muffle the laugh threatening to burst free. "On second thought, maybe we should have something to cool us down."

He emerged with a bottle of champagne. Inspecting the bottle, he declared, "Ah! Perfect! Quality but at an affordable price. Just as I'd expect from one of my top economists." Smiling widely as she opened her mouth to protest, he swiftly popped the cork and directed her to fetch some flutes.

"Honestly, what are you *doing*? We are not celebrating!" Devon rounded on him with the glasses, looking adorably flustered and out of sorts.

Bennett concentrated on pouring the champagne while hiding a grin.

"Sure we are. Here, take it." He handed her a glass, then tapped the rims and waited for her to sip.

"To the beginning of you and me." She gasped, but he continued. "And the end of your cotton panties."

Choking, Devon slammed her glass down. "You insufferable ass! We haven't *begun* anything, you—" stuttering, she came to a halt, unable to finish when he pressed a finger to her lips while laughing over the rim of his champagne.

"On the contrary. You think you know why I called a halt tonight, but you're wrong. We both know you would have regretted frantic sex on your couch." At her attempt to speak, he pushed his finger more firmly against her lips. "And *I* would have too. No, Devon. Our first time together will be as special as the occasion deserves. As *you* deserve. And this *is* the beginning for us. Believe it." Leaning over, he replaced his finger with the soft promise of a kiss.

Before she could respond, the kitchen door swung open, startling them both.

Standing in the doorway, with her white bra dangling from his finger, Dominic Martin looked from Devon to Bennett. "*I hope I'm not interrupting?*"

CHAPTER EIGHT

"JUST WHAT THE HELL WERE you *thinking?*"

A full day had passed. While not exactly calm, Devon no longer felt as bloodthirsty towards Dominic, a man she'd known most of her life. He stood near the exact spot where he'd flippantly destroyed her evening. Last night, she'd seen his satisfied smile when Bennett stormed out in a fury of explosive misunderstanding. She wanted an explanation.

He fidgeted. "Personally, I don't think you should be on a high horse. After all, it was *your* bra, no? In the sitting room? I was gentleman enough not to mention your panties, but I really think John raised you better than—"

He didn't get to finish the thought before Devon smacked her palm, hard, across his cheek. His face jerked to the side before he had time to catch himself. Gratified, she eyed the reddening mark. Her tone was quiet, belying the force of her slap and the fire darkening her eyes to pewter. "What *business*, what *right* do you think *you* have to come in here to judge or criticize me?"

Rubbing the imprint she'd left, he avoided her eyes. Pacing away, he strode over to the nearest window to gaze out before turning back to her. His chest rose on a deep breath before he answered. "Because I *love* you. I don't want you to get hurt." He returned to her, clasping her shoulders to stare into her eyes.

She sighed, holding him off. This was a conversation long overdue.

She'd been focused all her life. Gifted with numbers, and eager to please, she'd first devoted herself to family. Her particular skills worked well, it turned out, with their particular goals. Later, she'd continued to help while shifting her attention to school, knowing she wanted a different future for herself someday.

Now, she was on the way to that future, out of the game. But all of that single-minded attention had come at a cost. There'd been no time for Devon, not as a woman.

Her family saw her as naive, sheltered.

She choked back a laugh. In personal matters, yes. But she wondered if Bennett would see her as innocent if he really knew her.

Dominic shifted, calling her attention back to him.

"Listen to me. I'm not a child anymore. You can't walk in here and treat me like one." She reached up a finger to press his chin down so he'd meet her eyes. "I'm a grown woman, Dom. You've made things very awkward for me."

"Devvie, I'm sorry. I really am. You threw me off. I only want the best for you. I don't know this guy." His face was reddened, but no longer from her slap. "I don't see how *you* can know this guy very well. You've only been over here about five minutes." When she looked at him in reproach, he shifted again, slipping his hands into his pockets. "Give me a break. You're like a sister to me."

Reluctantly amused in spite of her frustration, she patted his arm. His hangdog expression reminded her of the time he'd knocked her out of a tree when they were ten. She'd broken her wrist and milked his guilt for all she could get. If memory served, she'd bagged her first iPod.

But she could never sustain being angry with Dominic for any real length of time. It appeared this would be no exception. He was family, and no matter how far she moved away, her loyalty was fierce. That didn't mean he was completely off the hook.

"Oh, all right, enough with the sackcloth and ashes. But I should make you apologize to Bennett. Otherwise, I don't know what he must be thinking."

"Wait. *What* did you say his name was?"

It was Devon's turn to look embarrassed and awkward.

"Bennett," she mumbled.

"Speak up, Devvie. Because I'm not sure I heard you." Dom's voice was stern, hard.

"Bennett. *Bennett Sterling*, okay?" She said it loudly, staring him down.

Dominic walked out of the kitchen, leaving her to gape after him before following closely behind. She trailed him into the sitting room, watching as he paced the length of the small room twice before slumping onto the couch, legs sprawled.

"Please tell me you didn't just say that."

"I can't." She eyed him as he looked anywhere but at her. "Don't you think you're overreacting just a little, Dom? I'm the one with the problem here. Thanks to *you*."

***

Dominic shook his head, cursing himself for not seeing that the man in Devon's kitchen last night had too much confidence and arrogance to be some average guy. It fit perfectly that he was Bennett Sterling. He was the man in charge of Sterling International, Devon's future, and if things progressed to plan, Dom's next client.

It was the worst kind of misfortune for Devon and Bennett to be involved.

Dominic narrowed his eyes on hers. "You need to stop this right now. You know better than to get involved with someone who has that kind of power over you." He leaned toward her, ignoring the headache starting to pound in his temple. At her continued silence, he said, "Are you hearing me, Devon?"

She was slowly shaking her head. Hugging herself, she said thickly, "It was like being flicked by lightning, Dominic, the day I met him." She looked around the room, vacantly. "And I haven't been the same since." Meeting his eyes again, he was struck by the moisture glossing over the colorless gray. "I don't think I ever will be," she added.

Feeling slightly panicked at the certainty in her voice, he grabbed her hand. "No, Devvie. You're just inexperienced, that's all."

She smiled faintly. "I thought so too. But it doesn't seem to be going away." She put her hand over his, squeezing lightly. "And maybe it *is* just a passing attraction. I'm certainly entitled to one. You've had your share. Dad's even had his. Everyone has dated and been *normal*, at least in that way, except *me*." She choked out a rusty laugh. "I'm being fanciful about him. I'd really just like to explore this. Have a little fun before it ends. God knows, it *will* end."

Dominic paused. "Why do you say that?"

At her questioning look, he clarified. "Why do you say it *will* end? As if it must? You don't know that."

Her brows lowered, puzzled. She started to rise, then sat again, smiling a little lopsidedly. "Because it does. It would. You know that." She looked at him in genuine confusion.

Dominic forgot about the plans, the project, and the need to discourage her from Bennett Sterling. He'd had no idea, even after all these years. Pulling her closer, he hugged her with one arm but she stared at the floor. "This is about your mother. Angeline."

She stiffened, but didn't pull away. After several long moments, she spoke. "Maybe. I don't know, I don't think about her. I don't even remember her. She left when I was four. And you know she never looked back. Dad said she must not have been able to handle it. Us. So she left." She stumbled to a halt.

He tugged a strand of her hair, as he'd been doing since she was five years old and he was seven. She looked up into his eyes.

"That doesn't mean everyone leaves, Devvie. I would never leave you, little sister. And neither would your father. My parents stayed together until cancer *made* my mother leave. You just had the bad luck to get a mom that couldn't stick. That's on her. Don't give up on everyone else."

He tweaked her chin, then gave it a little pinch, just because of that earlier slap. "Have fun with your Bennett. Lightning doesn't strike twice, you know." He sent up a silent prayer that nothing serious would come of it.

The doorbell interrupted anything she might have said. She squeezed his waist, and then rose to go answer the door. "Thank you, Dom."

He nodded, waiting until she was completely gone. With a heavy sigh, he leaned his head back against the couch, reassessing. Hearing the faint murmur of voices, he made a quick decision.

He walked into the kitchen to avoid anyone, checking the time on his watch. When he was content to hear Devon walking into the sitting room with her visitor, he pulled his cell phone from his back pocket. It would give him time to make his call.

After a couple of rings, his father, Patrick Martin, answered.

Dominic leaned a hip against the counter, frowning. "Dad? We might have a problem here."

***

"It is a great and generous God that puts two beautiful women in the same room at the same exact time." Dominic leaned in the doorway, holding a bottle of wine with two glasses.

Devon briefly closed her eyes then cast a silent signal of gratitude skyward. "Dominic," she exclaimed. "I was wondering where you'd gone off to. Let me introduce Natalie Enfeld." She gestured to her guest with a hand. "She's Bennett's PA and she's here to pick up a few things for the office. Natalie, this is Dominic Martin, an old family friend."

Natalie had shown up, unannounced, to get some files for Bennett. When asked why it couldn't wait until Monday, or whether Devon could help at all, the woman had clammed up. Maybe Dominic could lighten the atmosphere.

He set the wine and glasses down on the coffee table before stepping forward to greet the petite blonde. Devon observed as Natalie hovered near the fireplace, shyly gawking.

Devon swallowed a laugh. Natalie Enfeld was speechless, staring at Dominic like a love-struck girl. It was easy for Devon to forget his initial impact on people, especially women. Pouring herself some Chardonnay, Devon settled into a seat to enjoy the show.

"Hello Natalie. It's a pleasure to meet you." Dominic held out his hand in greeting. "May I pour you some wine?"

Taking his hand, Natalie stirred herself to answer. "Hello. Oh, no, please don't let me interrupt! Well, I know I'm interrupting, but I'll just be leaving so you two can get back to your evening." She cast a meaningful glance between Devon and Dominic, clearly curious. "And I can see you only have two glasses, so, well—"

Dominic interjected. "Natalie, you're not interrupting. Devon and I have plenty of time to catch up. Besides, she's like my little sister. We'll be on each other's nerves within fifteen minutes." He looked to Devon and she smiled in agreement.

"I'm sure we have another glass. I'm equally sure Dev would be happy to get it. Right Devvie?"

Devon was fascinated. Frankly, she'd never seen Natalie as anything less than perfectly composed, physically or verbally. Within minutes of meeting

Dominic, she was rambling, mumbling a little, and nervously tugging her sweater hem. She looked positively relieved when Dominic pointed out that Devon was purely platonic, sister material.

"Yes." Devon sprung up from the couch. "I'll just be a moment, please excuse me."

She hurried from the room, shaking with laughter. Returning with the extra glass, she was back in time to hear Natalie stammering a refusal to Dom's persistent hospitality. She'd taken Devon's seat on the couch.

"No, well, thank you, but I can't." Huffing out a deep breath, she startled when Devon set the additional glass on the table. "Oh I really must be going." She scrambled to her feet, fumbling her cuff back to check her watch. "Oh, really. I... well. Bennett is expecting me. I'm only here to pick up this file." She bent to pick up the discarded folder that Devon had given her earlier. "And now I have it. So, I'll be going." She turned, only to briefly tangle in the straps of her handbag, which was lying near her feet.

Dominic was up and behind her, steadying her with one arm braced at her waist. "Whoa there. Steady on, Natalie."

Flustered, she said, "I need to go. Bennett is leaving town and he needs this file."

Devon sobered, all humor extinguished. "Oh. And are you going with him?" She bit her lip, knowing Natalie might chew into her for asking questions. Or clam up as she had before.

Natalie turned to the other woman, looking slightly dazed, still standing with one of Dom's hands pressed lightly to the small of her back. "No. Actually, he's leaving on this trip alone and won't be returning for at least a week. He'll keep me aware of his movements as needed."

Dominic chose that moment to lightly cup Natalie's elbow, capturing her attention. Devon nodded, offering a two-finger salute behind the other woman's back for his assistance.

"Well, let's get you gathered up, then." He picked up Natalie's handbag, deftly slipping it onto her shoulder. Then he took the file, straightening its contents before handing it back, ordered and neat. He smiled down at her, genially.

A small line creased between Natalie's brows as she looked her fill of Dominic. She began speaking again, as if someone had prompted her. "It's not so unusual, really. Sometimes he's known to take unexpected trips, on his own, just like this one. Occasionally a last minute detail pops up somewhere that he wants to take care of personally. Or he has a project in its infancy that needs his full focus and attention."

Devon nodded, even though Natalie wasn't watching her at all, she was in fact ogling Dominic. "Thank you. It's nice of you to let me know what's happening. And explain what's normal." Devon walked to the doorway, prompting Dominic to begin herding the other woman into the foyer.

As they all moved into the small space, it occurred to Devon that Natalie had never been this gracious or accommodating to her. She'd been polite, and professional, but always distant. Even a little cold.

She followed the other woman's eyes as they traced Dominic's movements behind them.

He stepped close, gently prying loose the fingers Natalie had clutched around the strap of her bag. Bringing her knuckles to his lips, he bussed a quick kiss against them while grinning down at her. He brought her hand down, but kept her fingers in his.

Devon marveled at the exchange.

"It was a pleasure meeting you. And Ms. Enfeld?"

Stirring herself, Natalie answered, "Yes?"

"I'm only here for a short visit, but I'd love to see Devon's workplace, your workplace, meet everyone. Would you be bothered," he lightly squeezed her hand, "if I dropped in for a visit?"

Stammering a little, she replied, "No, of course, well, no, of course not." She smiled and stepped back, bumping the doorway. "No. We'd be delighted to have you visit, Mr. Martin. Please just arrange it with Devon and I'll, I mean, she'll or we'll…" She stopped, taking a breath. "Someone will take you around for introductions and a quick tour." She straightened, and resolutely freed her hand. With one last wan smile, she turned to face the exit.

"Thank you. I'll do that." Smiling charmingly, Dominic reached around, brushing her waist to open the door for her. "I look forward to seeing you again soon."

"Yes, I— of course." Blushing, she firmly gathered herself and turned to Devon. "I'll see you at the office."

Closing the door, Devon leaned back against it, looking up at Dominic through her lashes. "What exactly are you up to?"

Lounging against the wall, Dominic looked back innocently. "Can we go back and sit down? I really want that drink." He turned without waiting for her reply, ambling off.

Devon followed to find he'd already resumed his seat on the sofa, and he handed over her glass of white wine as she sat beside him. She held the glass, waiting.

"You've really gotten soft, you know."

Swiveling her head, she asked, "What?"

"Correct me if I'm mistaken, but you wanted information about Bennett. From Ms. Enfeld." Holding up a hand as she started to interrupt, he continued. "If I'm not further mistaken, there seems to be some mild tension between you and Natalie. In the spirit of cooperation and familial loyalty, I decided to distract her for you. And you got the information you wanted without her freezing up." He grinned, leaning back while propping his leg on the opposite knee. "So, you're welcome, Devvie. Really, have you forgotten everything you ever learned?"

Devon leaned forward to set her wine on the table, untouched. She clasped her hands in her lap, contemplating him.

"Forgive me, Dominic. I've been remiss. *Thank you.*" She reached over to pat his knee with a false smile. "But I'd hardly need to wonder where Bennett is if it weren't for your interference in the first place. And I haven't gone so soft that I don't smell another game in play."

Dom shifted back, looking wounded. "Now you're being paranoid, and that would hurt if I didn't know you're a little off balance right now." He patted her cheek in feigned comfort. "A little loyalty, sister, hmm?"

***

"Well, does anyone know when he *will* be returning?" Devon knew she sounded impatient, but couldn't keep the helpless frustration she felt from leaking into her voice. "He's been gone for days and the only person that seems to know anything is Natalie."

Aidan glanced up from his laptop. "Devon, I know you're restless, but it's just the way Bennett does things sometimes. He goes offsite and offline to work on a problem until he has a handle on it. Communications are kept to a minimum so there are limited to no interruptions. Believe it or not, it's effective and usually brings him back sooner than later."

Sighing, she propped a hip on his desk, edgy with tension. For days, she'd been trying to work out exactly what *problem* Bennett was struggling to solve. She'd been steadfast in her refusal to believe he'd simply walked out on her, leaving her alone. She wanted her chance to explain, recapture the closeness they'd found before Dominic's interruption.

He'd said it was a beginning, *their* beginning.

But he hadn't called or texted. Not even an email. The most optimistic of people would consider his disappearance ill timed.

Devon wasn't feeling optimistic.

She looked up to see Aidan watching her, his gaze level. She said, "I wish he'd consider talking to one of us. It's frustrating relaying information back and forth with Natalie as his only liaison."

Aidan patiently listened, not saying anything. Uncomfortable with his unblinking observation, she looked down, inspecting her nails one by one. At his continued silence, she briskly rubbed her arms before finally meeting his eyes.

"*What?*"

"You need to ease off Natalie, Devon. Your personal bias is showing through. She's his assistant. Why wouldn't he communicate with her? Why would he talk to us instead?" He paused, frowning. "What do you have against her?"

She gathered herself, straightening.

Ruefully, she said, "Nothing." When Aidan raised his brows, she repeated it. "*Nothing.* I'm sorry. I'm not myself. I don't like it when I don't know what's happening." She forced a laugh. "Maybe I'm a control freak." She clasped his forearm in quick reassurance. "Forgive me. Anyway, we have much more important things to discuss." She beamed at him, confident it would cut the current of tension in the room.

He automatically smiled back. He asked, "What's that?"

"Jane! What was her answer? *Did she say yes?*"

***

Devon returned upstairs, upbeat about Aidan and Jane's good news despite her own personal worries. Happiness smothered the small smack of guilt from guiding Aidan away from topics best not explored.

But really, what man didn't want to talk about himself a little? Or his love life?

Aidan was a good friend besides being an exceptional director. Devon didn't like to think she was manipulating him.

Old habits died hard.

It was exactly why she preferred this world, with its ethical precision over the murky ambiguity of her past. And her family's *current* domain, if everything were the same. She had no reason to believe anything had changed. They'd forged a pact to not speak of it, because she worried. And she'd moved on. So had Dominic, she'd believed. That had been the plan.

But maybe not.

Something about his actions around Natalie smacked of ulterior motives. Devon wasn't so far removed that she couldn't still catch a whiff of something *off.* She frowned, wondering if her instincts were still accurate and true.

If so, a game was afoot.

At the sound of the elevator doors opening behind her, Devon snapped her head around, hoping it was Bennett. Instead, Natalie walked toward her, briskly appointed in a stunning aubergine skirt with jacket. Her blonde hair was loosely coiled up, and rather than her normal discreet diamond studs, she wore gold hoops and stacked bracelets. She vibrated with color. Devon stared at the transformation.

"Is my slip showing, Devon?"

Devon gathered herself, and stated the bare truth. "No, you look wonderful."

"Thank you. And do I normally look so bad?"

The woman tried Devon's patience to its limit, but there was no need for bad manners. Or unprofessionalism. Aidan's earlier comments had stung.

When confronted with the truth, no matter how uncomfortable, Devon never avoided penance. Ruefully, she acknowledged her sins and set about correcting them. Smiling through gritted teeth, she answered the other woman. "No, of course not. But this is a little different from what you normally wear. And it's lovely."

There was something else different about Natalie, something besides new clothing and accessories. Devon couldn't quite put her finger on it.

The elevators returned once again. Both women watched as Dominic walked out, innate confidence in his stride. Stopping between the two women, he looked from one to the other before addressing Natalie. A rosy flush washed into the apples of her cheeks before receding to pale pink.

"Ms. Enfeld. It's a pleasure to see you again so soon."

***

He was clad in dark denims and boots. A fitted black sweater contrasted exquisitely with the burnished gold of his hair. Absently, she noticed a loose wave curling onto his forehead above mossy green eyes that crinkled in the corners. Amusement glimmered there and in the slight curve of his mouth as he eyed her up and down. His strong jaw was smooth, the light stubble he'd sported the last time they'd met shaved away.

Put simply, Dominic Martin was a stunning man.

She blinked rapidly before forcing herself to step forward and hold out her hand, "Mr. Martin. How are you today?"

"Wonderful. I'm finding London to be beautiful, Natalie, in unexpected places."

Taking a quick breath, she tugged her hand from his where he still held it. He was too attractive for his own good, and seemed to know it. But he was so relentlessly charming, she found herself excusing his vanity, reluctantly attracted.

She paused on the thought, involuntarily remembering Bennett and that last evening together. Along with its disastrous ending.

She'd been having a lovely time, viewing art, before going to enjoy wine and dinner at the chic little bistro pub he co-owned. In full denial, she'd told herself Bennett was more like he used to be before the past few months.

Before Devon.

Natalie had flirted, lightly, determined to win back his favor. And that's when he'd spelled it all out, in clear and plain English. He cared about Natalie as a friend. Nothing more.

Never anything more.

She'd sat there, numb. When she'd roused herself to speak, point out the ways they could be a perfect couple, his attention had already wandered.

To Devon, sitting right there in the same pub, at the bar, drinking alone.

He watched her.

He walked to her. Talked to her. Ultimately, he'd chased after her.

Natalie was left with the barest of apologies and a credit card to cover the tab and her cab fare home.

The humiliation still stung. She'd been an utter fool. She had no idea what transpired since then to send Bennett off in the foulest of moods, but it didn't change anything. It was nothing to do with her. It was all Devon. Bennett was upset because of *Devon*.

None of it was anything to do with Natalie.

For a week, she mourned losing him. But the fact was, Natalie had never *had* Bennett Sterling. In the time she'd worked for him, her feelings had grown, complicating their relationship. His feelings had not.

Unexpectedly and irrationally, she felt a sudden lightness.

Letting out a slow breath, she switched her attention to Dominic, running her eyes over him. This was a virile male, primed and interested. He quirked a brow up at her perusal, meeting her eyes before conducting his own survey up and down the length of her. She was sure she caught a glint of conspiracy in his eyes.

"You know, Natalie, you can get quite a snobby look there. Are you a toff?"

She burst out in laughter before she could stop herself. "A *what?*"

His eyes crinkled up as he grinned. "A toff. You know an upper class, society type."

Determined, she stepped up to him, crowding right up so she was within inches of him, face to face. Gratified when confusion briefly clouded his gaze, she almost missed the tiny movement he made to step back before catching himself. She reached up a hand, brushing a lock of dark golden hair from his brow before lightly tapping her finger on his nose.

"I know what it means. It's short for *toffee-nosed.*" A satisfied smile slowly spread across her face. "But I don't mind if you call me *Toff.*" Stepping around to link her arm through his, she turned to see Devon gaping. "Devon, I'll take Mr. Martin here on a tour. Maybe we'll step out for some coffee too." She looked at Dominic and he nodded in affirmation. "I'll bring him back to you later."

As they walked away together, Natalie took a deep breath, catching the faint citrus of Dominic's cologne. So different than Bennett's.

Suddenly, she felt good, powerful, and decisive.

She wouldn't be a fool again.

***

Bennett stepped into his office, unnerved by the silence. He'd encountered no one so far, not on his floor anyway. And somehow, illogically, he'd expected to see some difference, an evidence of his absence. Instead, things were pristine, as neatly organized as ever.

Ten days ago, he'd left in a haze of fury and rage. There had been no choice, no other avenue except escape. He hadn't trusted himself to stay.

Already he'd done things completely foreign to his character. Bennett prided himself for his control. He didn't force himself inside apartments. Kiss women in anger. Become lovers with staff.

Never that. Not since Olivia. She'd taught him well enough to keep pleasure out of business. To be wary when passion and trust ran wild. God knows she'd burned him badly.

He'd been a boy really, looking back. Devastated with grief from the sudden loss of his parents. Overwhelmed by the reins of Sterling International being thrust upon him. And rather than the love and support he'd expected, Olivia had chosen that moment to betray him. She'd left him for the competition. Another man, another company. Because he'd trusted her and she'd worked by his side, she'd taken a hefty sum of accounts and clients with her.

He'd reminded himself of these lessons while he was away. Now, over a week later, he felt reasonably calm again. He was resolved, determined. He would take back control and stop the undisciplined chaos his life had become. Walking further into the room, he headed for the window and its skyline view.

And saw her.

Devon stood there, straight and slim, arms hugging her waist as she faced away. Unaware of him, she stared out, completely still. He had the distinct impression that she was wholly, entirely vulnerable.

Strangely unsure of himself, Bennett turned to quietly leave her. But she heard him, peering over her shoulder with darkened eyes that looked unbearably lost before she veiled them.

She searched his face. The decisions and resolutions of the past days mocked him, daring him to step closer, move forward until his body could collide with hers.

His control strained. Swearing softly under his breath, hands fisted in his pockets, he took a deliberate step backwards.

Her eyes flashed before clearing like mist. He saw the subtle squaring of her shoulders while she dropped her hands to hang loosely at her sides. His composure stuttered as she gathered hers around her in motionless, silent dignity. Pain pierced him, somewhere near his heart.

Dully, she said, "You're back."

CHAPTER NINE

BENNETT PUSHED DOWN THE ACHE, reminding himself of what was best. Waving a hand for her to join him, he sat down behind his desk. "Devon, please take a seat. I'd like a word."

She folded herself gracefully into the chair he'd motioned to, then crossed her feet beneath her. She looked at him expectantly. "Yes?"

"I know I left abruptly, but I'd like to clear the air between us now that I'm back." At her silence, he went on. "I've thought things over, and I realize I blurred the boundaries between us. It's more than past time I set things right."

Some emotion rippled across her face, then was gone.

He paused, but when she failed to speak, he continued. "I own this business and you're an employee. We each need to respect who and what we are. And we should forget anything from when we might have confused those basic relationships."

She was pale as marble. "Is it…" Her voice was raspy, and she stopped, clearing her throat. She looked somewhere over his shoulder, out the window. "Is it Natalie?"

"What?"

More firmly, she asked, "Is it Natalie? Are you involved with her? You were out together that one night. When we…" Her voice trailed off.

"No!" He repeated it, more firmly. "No." No matter what, she mustn't think that. "It's… I never date employees, Devon. I made a mistake once, a long time ago and it cost me dearly." Her eyes swung back to his, a clear misty gray. The ache throbbed.

He needed to carry this through to the end; otherwise he'd do something irrational like ask her about the man who'd been at her flat. What he was to her, how he mattered. He wasn't sure he could bear the answer.

He took a deep breath, steeling his resolve. "We are not good for each other, Devon. No matter what has come before, for me or you, we are terrible now. I am not myself around you. And I suspect you're not at your best either."

Again, she said nothing. Just a tiny shake of her head while her hands lay clasped in her lap, seemingly relaxed. But Bennett could see her knuckles straining white.

Absently, he rubbed his chest. "Are we agreed then?" He rose, signaling the end of their talk. Of everything.

With a short nod, she rose. She hesitated, as if unsure what to do for a second, before visibly straightening. Pasting on a small, superficial smile, she smoothed her skirt with steady hands then turned and walked out. He barely heard the door close behind her.

Bennett convinced himself the lingering pain was relief, rather than regret.

***

Devon was in the stairwell before the shaking started.

She sat down on a step, hugging herself hard as she tried to contain the hurt leaking out of her. She trembled, weakly leaning against the wall as pain punched its way into her, stealing her breath.

He hadn't even asked about Dominic. Who or what he was to her.

She'd been prepared to apologize. Argue first. Accuse him of jumping to conclusions. Then concede how badly things might have looked, ask forgiveness, and have fun making amends. Fool that she was, she'd believed him when he'd said they were starting something new. A relationship. She never thought a simple misunderstanding would derail them so quickly.

He'd said it was a beginning.

With a sinking stomach, she realized she was in deeper than she thought.

She *wanted* him to care. *Needed* him to want her enough to fix this. But he couldn't. Something had happened a long time ago; an old bruise that shuttered his eyes, barricaded his heart, and closed him away from her.

She wouldn't pick at him, opening a wound that clearly hadn't healed. She deserved better, for one thing. And he should heal himself, come to someone whole on his own someday.

Someone equal to him.

His talking about her place, and his, had smarted. She fully understood he was the boss, she the employee. But the differences keeping them apart went far deeper.

She'd been deluded for a brief time, giddy from their evening, thinking she could talk to him. Share her past. First by talking about Dominic, and then the rest of her family. Herself. But he'd reminded her, unintentionally yet forcefully, of what was important. And what she couldn't forget again.

I can never have Bennett Sterling.

A small gasp escaped. It was getting harder, not easier to repeat the mantra she'd enlisted all those weeks ago. Was she in love with him?

No.

She refused the idea. With pain filled eyes, she looked down at the stairs where she sat, seeing where her tears spattered the concrete. She so rarely cried; it disoriented her for a second. Then she sobered, straightening.

No. She had been falling for him.

Pausing, she accepted that, knowing it for the terrible error it was.

Because he doesn't love me. He couldn't for one thing. And he wouldn't. He was clear about that.

Devon sat until her legs began to tingle, numb from the prolonged inactivity. Her tears dried, although her lungs ached with what she hadn't shed. But now wasn't the time to overthink any more than she had already. There wasn't any point.

It wouldn't change anything.

Just as she had a right to her own feelings, Bennett had a right to his. No matter how painful, and how difficult, she must accept that. Mustering up her spirit, she rose, straightening her stiff body.

Things could be worse. Bennett *hadn't* asked any questions. And she'd offered no excuses, no explanations. At least she could salvage her pride, bruised though it may be. After all, Bennett probably thought she was involved with the man who'd interrupted them. *Dominic.*

She had to find him. She knew Dom was casually flirting with Natalie, flattering and charming her. They'd shared at least one coffee. But whatever Dom's interest in the other woman, it could only be superficial. He could end whatever he'd begun there as fast as he'd started it.

Devon needed him as a front, a salve to her pride. Let Bennett assume his worst about them. Dom owed it to Devon to do this. Part of this mess she was in was his fault, she rationalized. He'd been the catalyst. Now he would help her walk away with some degree of self-respect.

It would benefit them both. After all, Natalie was like Bennett, and they were different from people like Dominic and Devon. Their worlds might touch professionally, but never privately.

Yes, Dominic should leave Natalie alone. That way, Natalie could go back to where she belonged.

Just as Devon would.

***

Dominic pushed the reluctant blonde into the cab before ducking in after her, laughing. Throwing an arm around her waist, he leaned in to press a kiss to her lips but found a smooth cheek instead, cool from the outdoor autumn air. Fall had descended on London in the past weeks, charming him with its rainy gloom and soggy fallen leaves. Breathing in Natalie's floral perfume, he nuzzled her ear and caressed the area beneath her breast, outside the gabardine trench she wore.

Natalie leaned back, avoiding him. "Dominic!" She softly hissed, while melting against him.

He slipped his hand beneath her jacket, chafing her nipple through the fine silk of her blouse while watching the driver to make sure his exploits went unnoticed. She whimpered, and he cut off the sound with his mouth. Moving back, he waited until she opened her eyes to look at him. "Yes?" As she flushed, he winked lecherously and pinched her hip.

As always, she couldn't hold back a grin. He loved the fact he could draw out any mood, any response in her. She was fantastic.

"You're incorrigible. But why are you rushing me into this cab?"

Sobering, he straightened. Still keeping an arm looped loosely around her shoulders, he lightly squeezed. "Because Bennett was back there. I was afraid he'd see us."

She considered him for a long moment. "Tell me, again, why we don't want anyone to know we're seeing each other? Because I seem to have forgotten. I mean, we're both single, we should be free to do as we please. Why are we sneaking around?"

Dominic knew how to take the measure of other people. He'd grown up learning how to do it and it was second nature to him now. But women would always elude perfect prediction.

Gently, he reached up to Natalie's brow and tucked a stray strand of hair behind her ear. He let his fingers linger, caressing the sensitive area along her nape until he reached the loose chignon she favored. He didn't muss it, as he longed to. Instead he regretfully dropped his hand to clasp one of hers.

"I told you all I could. Things got a little complicated between Devon and Bennett. She needs my support. As family. She's like a little sister to me, Toff, for real." Natalie dipped her chin and no longer met his eyes. He dropped his head down until he captured her gaze again.

"I mean it Nat. Devon is important to me, but as family. You have to believe that. I'm not cheating you. Since I couldn't give you up, I kept you secret instead." Before she could move away, he pressed his lips to hers in a quick kiss. He searched her face as he moved back, needing to know her thoughts.

Natalie was required to move his plan forward. She was integral.

When Devon had asked him to leave Natalie alone, he'd caved to her request. Devon had been so upset, more alone than he'd ever seen her. But he'd known he couldn't, wouldn't honor his word. The last thing he wanted was for Devon to find out he'd been seeing Natalie for weeks.

But Natalie's face told him all he needed to know. It was time to bluff.

"If it's this important to you, we can go talk to Devon right now. Hell, we'll talk to Bennett too. And anyone else you can think of." He saw relief lighten the cornflower blue of her eyes, and his stomach unknotted. "Tell you what, let's take out an ad in one of your fancy London papers. How's that? We'll announce ourselves." He brought the back of her hand to his lips.

Her response was immediate. "No, you idiot," she laughed. "I'm sorry. I was having a moment, that's all. I'm over it. And honestly, jealousy isn't something I'm usually prone to, I promise."

He was genuinely puzzled. "So why now?"

She blushed. "Well, you're gorgeous, for one." She rolled her eyes as he hammered it up, shaking his hair back and leering. "And I'm crazy about you."

Dominic winked, but his stomach dropped.

Natalie moved closer, smiling up through her lashes at him. "Plus, you're pretty good at sneaking around. I think you might be a rogue." She bit his chin in a saucy tease before raising her lips for a kiss.

Dominic leaned down, meeting her mouth.

In seconds, all his doubts were lost in the beautiful match they made.

***

Bennett watched the cab pull away with Natalie and Dominic crouched low, laughing like conspirators. He'd suspected for more than a week now that the two might be involved, after having met Mr. Martin in the offices one day. He'd been outside Bennett's office, with Devon nowhere in sight. Natalie had supplied the introductions, not picking up on the tense exchange between the two men. She'd been abnormally occupied with Dominic, he'd thought.

Now he knew why.

Gladness bubbled up inside him.

After weeks of misery and sleepless nights, he staggered in relief. Throwing his head back, he began to laugh. Devon wasn't involved with Dominic, she never had been. He'd been so certain, positive she was another Olivia.

He'd been an ass. It was blatantly obvious now, but he'd been blind. He'd punished her for the sins another woman had committed. And he couldn't have been more wrong.

Bennett set off walking. Wondering.

What else had he gotten wrong?

***

With a bag of groceries and bottle of wine, Bennett stood smiling on his grandfather's stoop when Charles Sterling opened the door. Walking inside, Bennett led the familiar way back to the kitchen, taking a moment to hand his grandfather his coat before settling his purchases on the marble counter.

"You're back in town, I see."

Bennett nodded, still smiling, while he busied himself fishing out a corkscrew from a nearby drawer. Grabbing two glasses, he opened the wine and poured before answering.

"Yes. I'm glad to be back, wanted to catch up with you. How about a fire before I fix up dinner?" It was gloomy and damp outside, despite the midsummer season.

Bennett continued to make himself at home by crossing to the small sitting area that was nestled within a nook beside the kitchen. Taking some wood from a recess in the wall, he stacked it in the small grate. Crouching low, he lit the kindling until it caught, pausing a moment to watch the flames flicker.

He turned, finding that his grandfather had already taken one of the seats flanking the fire. He sat in the other before picking up his wine from the small table beside him.

"Now what if I'd had a date tonight?"

Bennett looked at his grandfather in surprise. He typically planned his visits, to be polite. But he'd been so caught up in his thoughts, it never occurred to him not to arrive unannounced. "Are you seeing someone?" The thought was disturbing, somehow. Surely, no one could ever replace his grandmother. Yet his grandfather deserved happiness and Rose Sterling was gone.

"No, I'm teasing. And you can take that look off your face, Bennett. I haven't started seeing anyone. Although I'd be open to the possibility, so you must accept that."

Bennett took a long drink of wine, staring into the fire. "I know it's irrational, but it's hard to think anyone could ever measure up. You'd never be satisfied, would you?"

Charles closed his eyes, as if recalling an image or memory. But when he opened them again, they were bright and lively. Quietly, he said, "We can't stop living, Bennett. And that's what happens when you dwell in the past. You deny the present and every possibility it offers. And the very worst crime you can commit against another person is to compare them to another. We're all individuals, with our strengths, our weaknesses. But we *are* unique. Don't take that away from someone."

Bennett leaned forward, his attention sharpened on every word. Understanding dawned on his face. "You're right. God, you're right again,

Granddad." He relaxed, slumping back into the cushioned seat. "How did you get so wise?"

His grandfather chuckled, "I'm always telling you I know everything. You should listen. Besides, I suspect you've been punishing yourself for a long time now. You've been denying yourself, closing people off. You felt you had something to atone for, Bennett. And you never did."

Bennett paused to take in what his grandfather was saying. It really was time he listened. "I've made a mess of things."

Charles cocked a brow.

"There's this woman. I told you a little about her, her name is Devon." Bennett laughed, remembering the conversation. Charles had openly admired the spunk of a woman who'd throw a shoe at his grandson's prized profile.

Charles immediately caught on. "Ooh, the feisty one, yes?" At Bennett's rueful nod, he hooted in good humor. "Well done, boy! I've never told a living soul, but Rose bounced her purse off my skull when we were barely married. Caught me from behind, with my back turned. I've never seen a woman so angry when I assumed she'd be doing all the cooking and cleaning." He clutched a hand to his stomach, guffawing.

"You mean you didn't cook? I thought you loved it."

"I *learned* to love it. It was that or starve, but I do enjoy it now. As you know."

Shaking with laughter, Bennett rose to bring over the wine and top off their glasses. "I'll be damned. That's a great story, Granddad."

"She was a hell of a woman, Rosie. But I want to hear more about your Devon and what you've been up to." He stood, and before Bennett could protest, started unpacking the groceries. "Settle down and talk to me. I'm feeling nostalgic now for cooking and my kitchen. You sit and tell me everything I want to know."

Love for his grandfather swamped Bennett. There was no equal to Charles Sterling, and he'd give him anything he wanted. "Well, the first thing is that she's not *my* Devon. I've barely spoken with her for weeks." At Charles' puzzled look, he continued. "I told you I'd made a mess. It started with a misunderstanding. I jumped to conclusions, bad ones. I thought she was playing me for a fool, like Olivia had."

"Ah." There was a wealth of understanding in Charles' voice.

Bennett watched his grandfather expertly slide seasoned steaks into a sizzling hot pan. Not able to sit doing nothing, Bennett joined him to crack black pepper over a large bowl of torn salad greens. He casually tossed the whole bowl to mix the ingredients before turning to a fresh one where he started making a vinaigrette. They worked in tandem, long years in the kitchen together allowing for seamless harmony.

"So when do you plan to clean up this mess you've made? I assume you want to?"

"Yes." He broke off. Dazed, Bennett forgot to breathe as he stared at his grandfather in dumfounded wonder. *Where had his objections gone?*

"What?" Charles plated the steaks before taking the bowl of salad from Bennett's numb fingers. Adding portions of greens to each plate, Charles slid them over so they could sit at the island in the kitchen. He lined up napkins and cutlery, and filled both wineglasses while Bennett watched, mouth slightly open.

As Charles settled himself on his high-backed stool, he patted the one next to him in invitation.

"Come on, let's eat."

Bennett nodded his head, and then walked around the counter on jerky legs. He stared at his plate, a slow smile widening until it spread across his face.

"I know it's a good-looking steak, but what is going on with you?"

"Yes, I'm going to fix my mess, Granddad." Bennett let out a bark of laughter, grabbing his knife and fork. "Of course, it's partly her mess, too. She'll need to do some of her own fixing." Devon hadn't made a single attempt to correct the misconceptions he harbored about who Dominic might be. What he was to her.

Any man would have assumed the worst.

Charles hastily swallowed a bite of steak. "Now let me offer a little advice, Bennett."

"Hmm?" Bennett was upbeat now, eager to get things back on track.

"When it comes to women, sometimes it's best to fall on your sword. Take the fall, so to speak."

Bennett savored his steak, groaning his approval. "Granddad, you really are the best cook I know. I swear you could give some of London's best chefs a run for their money." He dabbed his mouth with his linen napkin before relishing a sip of wine. "Now don't worry, but Devon's a little different than most. She's very strong-minded. Volatile. And we need to start as we mean to go on. She really has acted poorly, now that I think of it."

Charles mumbled something, but Bennett couldn't quite catch it. "What was that, Granddad?"

"I think it's a good thing I've taught you how to cook. That's all."

Puzzled, Bennett cocked a brow. Sometimes Charles could be tangential, but he still seemed to have all his faculties.

His grandfather shook his head, reaching over to pat Bennett on the back of the hand. "Never mind. You'll learn everything soon enough. Here's to women."

Bennett raised his glass. "To women."

***

"Dominic, I finally have you to myself! I have no idea how you've been entertaining yourself, but I appreciate your independence. I've been a poor hostess." Devon grimaced as they walked from the tube to a connecting bus stop.

"Devvie, you're perfect. And you know I like being on my own. We'd kill each other if we were in each other's hip pockets." He squeezed her hand, sharing the old joke. They'd grown up with lots of time on their own, comfortable with no one or only each other as company. "But what is this incessant need you have to haul me around London on foot, tube, or train? Can't we grab a cab for crying out loud? It's not like we can't afford it."

He stopped in his tracks to complain, tugging Devon around by the hand until she faced him. Heaving a sigh, she patted his face. "I save all my old money, from before, in investments. You never know when you might need it and I don't have a multimillion dollar IT firm keeping me afloat." She pulled on him with her other hand, the one he still held captured. "Now, are you saying you're too delicate for public transportation? You sound like Natalie." She missed his arrested look, turning back toward the bus stop.

"What do you mean?" He dropped her hand, following in slower strides.

"Well, I doubt she sets foot in anything less than a hired taxi. You're the one that calls her *Toff*. I swear you're such a flirt. And she likes it." Grimly, Devon continued, anxious to catch the bus that would take them to the gardens in time to explore while there was good light.

After a quick hesitation, Dom teased in return, "Of course she likes it, Dev. Who wouldn't?"

Devon laughed, but only because she was meant to. "As long as you keep it to teasing, I don't care if you flirt with half of London. Just don't forget what I asked and what you promised. You're my cover. But the longer you're here, the more I worry about your libido."

He was saved from answering by the bus that pulled up to the curb. With a gentle hand to her back, Dominic urged Devon to board first. By the time they were settled in seats next to each other, the conversation dropped.

"Where exactly are you taking me?"

"City of London Cemetery gardens." Devon practically bounced on her seat, anticipating the ancient burial site. "You know how I love it."

"Good God, is that where we're going? Of all the sites in London, you haul me to a graveyard? You must have the same morbid fascination as ever. I had to drag you out of the old crypts around Savannah."

"I was hardly hanging about *inside* the crypts, Dominic. I just like the feel of the old places." Devon never shared why she'd begun visiting cemeteries as a young child. Not with anyone. Now, as an adult, it was true she'd developed an attachment to them over the years.

He looked at her for a long moment before linking hands again. "All right. I'll indulge your abnormal hobby. At least your mood's improved slightly. I was getting worried about you a week or so ago."

Devon looked out the window as the scenery passed by. "I accepted a few things. Bennett helped me remember some hard truths." She wheeled in her seat, facing Dom. "I know you thought I was being unreasonable at the time, but we're not for the likes of the Bennetts and Natalies of this world, Dom."

"What exactly do you mean?"

"You and I. We're different. We come from a different place they'd never understand."

"So we should live our lives alone?"

Devon furrowed her brow, thinking. "No, well, I don't know. I only know it would never have worked between Bennett and me. And you'd have wound up hurting Natalie." She stopped when Dominic frowned, squeezing her hand a little too hard. "You know you would have."

He slewed his eyes sideways to meet her gaze. "I know, Devon." A muscle in his jaw bunched. "I know."

***

Later that evening, Devon found herself alone again, Dominic having made some excuse to go out. She fought off the old familiar feelings of abandonment, telling herself she wasn't lonely. Restless, she wandered her flat. She'd picked up odd knick-knacks over the years since she was a young teen and earning some money.

She ran her hand over a smooth slice of agate from Georgia, admired her whimsical brass owl bookends. At the small table she'd fashioned as a working desk, she picked up a dainty white ceramic sleeping cat her father had bought her. It had been his answer to her repeated pleas for a pet.

Idly, Devon moved her index finger along the Persian's porcelain back. What was stopping her from getting a pet now? She quickly dismissed the idea, telling herself she was too busy, worked too many hours. The memory of her father's voice rang in her ears.

It would be a burden. We'd only have to leave it behind.

Devon winced, shying from the reminiscence. After that, she'd feared becoming a burden herself, so she'd made herself as useful as possible. And the thought of leaving something behind, something she loved, was so distressing she never mentioned a pet again.

She carefully replaced the kitten, walking away from the uncomfortable recollection.

Where had Dominic gone?

She paused. Being preoccupied with her own problems and Bennett, she hadn't been able to place her finger on it. But something seemed different about Dominic lately.

She plopped on the couch, picking up a cup of tea that had gone cold. Maybe it was her imagination. Maybe she was moping about, thinking too much, making up crazed scenarios. Really, what could he be up to?

He had a brilliant IT security business. He was hardly apt to risk that for far-fetched schemes she might dream up. It was more likely he was tucked away in a local cafe catching up with email and projects. She knew Dominic well enough to know he could work among tens of strangers with absolute focus, yet she drove him crazy simply by breathing in the same room.

So why was she suspicious?

She drained her cup, thinking. Sometimes when she came home, she'd get the impression he'd arrived just before she did. No matter that he might be lounging in the sitting room, shoes off, reading a book with a half empty glass of wine at his side. There was a restrained energy about him, simmering below the outward appearance of lazy calm.

He drummed his fingers in restless rhythms on the back of the sofa, something Dom never did. He was adept at being still, easy when others became tense or anxious. He considered it too revealing to make unconscious movements, or to say unnecessary things.

Devon's own thoughts sped as her adrenaline kicked up.

Sometimes he smelled different. There would be a freshness, like he'd been outside in the brisk autumn air. She'd rationalized it, not seeing why he wouldn't say so, rather than telling her he'd been inside all afternoon reading or relaxing.

And when she hugged him, like yesterday, she'd caught the scent of blooms, floral and greenly verdant. She'd remarked, but he'd dismissed it as a sample of travel shampoo he used.

But he was staying with her, sharing the products she stocked in the guest bedroom's bath. And those weren't flowery at all.

Was he seeing someone?

A knock at the door startled her out of her musings. Rising, she smoothed a hand over her hair before going to open the door. Taken unaware, she took a quick step backward before recovering her composure and grasping the door, still on its latch.

"Bennett. This is unexpected. What can I do for you?"

"For starters, you can let go of that door and let me in, Devon. Christ, I'm not here to murder you."

Irritation replaced surprise with swift efficiency. Shutting the door with a resolute click, she waited a full beat before unlatching and reopening it to Bennett's patient amusement. She turned on her heel, uncaring of manners.

"All right then, is this going to take long? Do you want something to drink?"

"How could I resist such a gracious offer? I'd love some wine."

Devon stared as he proceeded to walk into her kitchen and start opening random cupboards.

"Can I help you? What is it you're looking for?"

"Devon, I just told you. Some wine, a nice red if you have it. Please try to follow along."

She pushed a hand in front of him to close the cabinet he was busy looking into. With a sour look, she moved to a pantry and emerged with a corkscrew and an Italian red.

He simply grinned, taking both items from her and deftly uncorking the bottle. With a raised brow, he looked toward the cupboards again, but she intercepted him by fetching two glasses and pushing them towards him on the counter.

He poured both glasses and was walking out of the kitchen with them before she found her voice.

"Wait, where are you going?"

Turning back, he answered, "You didn't expect us to stand in your kitchen and drink these did you? Really Devon, let's be civilized." With that, he resumed walking into her sitting room where he took a seat on the sofa they'd shared so many weeks ago.

Devon sat in an armchair, several feet away.

Bennett smiled at her, benignly, before patting the seat next to his and gesturing at her wine, which he'd placed on the table in front of the sofa.

"Why don't you come a little closer? I won't bite."

She half-stood, awkwardly bending to reach for her wine while staying planted in front of her chair.

"No thank you, I'm fine where I am. Why don't you tell me why you're here?"

He crossed a leg while leaning back to eye her, one arm propped nonchalantly across the back of the sofa. He swirled his wine before taking a cautious sip, then smiled genially.

"Very nice," he decreed. "Aren't you having any?"

She gritted her teeth before impatiently tipping up her own glass and draining a quarter of the contents in one long swallow.

"Wonderful," she said flatly. "*Bennett, why are you here?*"

He set down his glass, giving her one long, level look. "I am here, Devon, because there's been a misunderstanding between us. It's time for it to end, so I'm not leaving until things are cleared up between us. In fact, I'm rather hoping I don't leave at all."

She sat back, staggered at his presumption.

"You and Dominic. Don't pretend to not know what I'm talking about."

"Why don't you explain, slowly, so I get it." A gradual burn warmed her body, working its way up.

He blithely ignored her sarcasm. "You let me believe there was something going on when there wasn't. I assumed the worst, yes, but you allowed it to go on longer than needed."

"And how exactly would I have spoken to you? You walked out, leaving this flat then the country by all accounts. Correct?" Her voice had steadily risen to an imperious demand.

"Because you had another man here! Anyone would have—"

"I'm not interested in what anyone would have done, Bennett." She sliced through his objections with pinpoint precision. "I was interested in *you*. But when *you* returned, after leaving me no opportunity to speak—"

"Now wait just a minute—"

She chopped the air with her hand, silencing him. "No, when you did return, you lectured me on *my place*." When his head flinched back, she went on, clearly on a roll. "Oh yes. *My* place, *your* place, and how working for you does not mean I am equal to you. Certainly not enough to mix *outside* Sterling International."

"Dammit, that is not true!"

"No, you know what? It doesn't even matter." Setting her glass down with a firm click, Devon rose and gestured toward the door. "You need to leave. I've heard enough, more than enough from you." She pressed a hand to her heart. "You were right before. You upset me and I don't like myself around you."

"No, if you would just listen to me for one minute."

"Don't you get it? You didn't listen to *me*. You wouldn't speak with me or see me. You *left*. So now you can leave again."

"What is this, Devon, some sort of payback? If you're expecting an apology, you must see that you're responsible for most of this entire mess. I mean—"

"*Bennett.*" He stopped, looking hard at her. Something in his navy eyes nearly made her weaken, tempted her to forget the explosive atmosphere. She swayed as energy crackled between them, tantalizing her with its heat. As he reached for her, she broke from his spell and jerked the front door open.

"*Get. Out.*"

***

She sat on the sofa, trembling, when Dominic returned. She'd moved both glasses so they sat in front of her, easier for her to judge the levels of wine in each. Methodically, she'd sip from first one and then the other, alternating so both drained downward equally.

Dominic hovered in the doorway, the muted light from the hall catching the golden lights in his dark blonde hair.

"You can come in, you know."

"Are you sure? This seems like a party for one."

She sighed, finally giving up the game by pouring the contents of one glass into the other. "Well that depends. Can you cheer me up?"

He walked in, shrugging off his coat to toss it over the arm of the chair she'd occupied earlier. He settled beside her, angling himself into the corner to look her in the eye.

"Talk to me. What happened today? I left you in a great mood, better than you've been in weeks. Or so I thought." He frowned. "And why are you drinking out of two wine glasses?"

"Bennett stopped by. Apparently, for some reason he's decided we did, in fact, have a colossal misunderstanding." She shot Dom a quick frown, silently blaming him for his role in the fiasco. "Bennett thought by conceding the mistake, and pointing out my responsibility for it, that we could make nice."

Devon eyed her glass. The wine was quite good and there wasn't much point in corking the small bit left in the bottle. Frankly, it was never as good later. Filling her glass past the polite level, she brought it to her lips.

Whatever her feelings for Bennett, she surely didn't *like* him much right now. He'd walked his arrogant self into her home, made himself comfortable, and declared the last agonizing weeks an unfortunate mix-up. And to top it off he said it was mostly her fault.

Then, he'd insulted her further by assuming he'd be spending the night. The man had no respect.

Dom cleared his throat, interrupting her runaway thoughts. "Devvie, you've been so sad these last few weeks. I've never seen you like this, you know."

She fidgeted, looking around the room before reluctantly meeting Dominic's questioning gaze. "Okay, yes. What's your point?"

"Look, I don't think it's a good idea for you to be involved with Bennett." He dropped his eyes then looked back up, resolve firming his voice. "But you're not happy and I hate that. Why didn't you fix this when he was here, and you had the chance?"

She stared, perplexed. "Because there's no point, Dominic." She sprung up to pace back and forth before coming back to sit again, picking up her glass to hold but not drink. "We're not suited, like I said."

"You spouted off a bunch of nonsense earlier today, Dev, and I let it go. But you don't actually believe we're less than anyone else do you?" When she hesitated, finally taking a drink of wine rather than answer him, he repeated himself. "*Do you?*"

"Yes," she hissed. She felt the flames of embarrassment heat her face, but continued. "I think most people, certainly people like Bennett, or Natalie for that matter, would never understand where we come from. They have no understanding of taking advantage of people, let alone for monetary gain, Dominic."

He slumped back on the sofa, astounded. "You're ashamed of us! Of yourself." She shook her head, but he overrode her. "No, you are. Well, we're going to clear this up right now, little sister." He reached over and took her face between his hands.

"You should be proud of our families. We made our own way, never asked anyone for anything. And both our fathers are well-respected members of Georgia society today. Hell, Savannah can't get enough of either one of them and you know how closed that city can be. Atlanta tries to claim them as favorite sons since they've based some of their business there. Come on, Devvie. They're legitimate entrepreneurs. Give them some credit."

Tears glazed her eyes, blurring Dominic's face in front of her. He was right. She'd refused to change her impressions and opinions of them even though her father and Dom's had continued to evolve as much as she. Dominic himself was world class in tech security, yet she'd been relegating him to concocted conspiracies and scams in her imagination.

She was ashamed.

Dominic wasn't finished. "And don't think your Bennett is a stranger to scandal either. It hasn't been that many years ago that he underwent a major upset with his investors. An employee took client accounts right from under his nose, fleeing with them to a rival firm. It took serious time and effort to repair the damage."

Devon absorbed that statement along with the rest. A shaky smile curved her lips and Dominic eased back, cuffing her gently under the chin. An awkward silence ensued, while each gave the other some space to think.

After several long minutes, Dom shifted to prop his elbows on his knees. Grabbing her glass, he took a drink before running his hand around his neck, loosening his collar.

"Devvie, just one more thing."

"Okay. Shoot."

"Explain what you meant by Bennett wanting to *make nice*."

Equally amused and exasperated, Devon burst out laughing. "Thank you."

"For what?"

"For being a jackass. You definitely cheered me up." Still chuckling, she scooted closer to lean against his bulk. "No, thanks for being you, Dom. You pointed out some hard truths I needed to hear."

He knocked his chin onto the top of her head. "I love you, little sister. Now don't stay up too late." He rose to leave her alone, tuned in to the fact she wanted to be.

"I love you too, Dommie." It was an old nickname, rarely used because he hated it.

He leaned down and twisted her earlobe in retaliation, just like when they were kids. She laughed, watching him walk out of the room. He really was better than any real brother could have been.

It wasn't until much later she realized he smelled like flowers.

CHAPTER TEN

Devon's illusions about family love and loyalty were shattered during an ordinary, if unscheduled, work break.

She and Aidan stepped out for coffee at a local café. Seeing Dom through the darkly paned windows that flanked the entrance, she grabbed at the door handle.

"Aidan, I can finally introduce you to my friend, Dominic," she exclaimed.

Aidan stopped her with a hand to her arm. He nodded toward the corner where a petite, icy blonde had joined Dominic.

Natalie.

Speechless, Devon watched as the couple engaged in an impassioned, if brief, kiss. She allowed

Aidan to lead her away, walking her down the street. She followed, unconscious of the people around them.

Numbly, she only thought of Dominic's promise. He'd sworn he wouldn't continue to see Natalie or pursue her. Devon had believed him, trusted in him to keep his word.

Why would he lie?

Aidan placed a hand to her back to lead her into a different coffee shop from any they'd frequented before. Finding a seat for her, he went to place their orders and returned moments later with two frothy cappuccinos.

"In lieu of scotch, I ordered you a triple shot of espresso. I hope that helps."

Looking into Aidan's kind, worried face, Devon smiled, albeit faintly, to reassure him.

"I'm sorry. I didn't expect to see that. I'm not sure how to react." She sipped her coffee, savoring the espresso as it echoed her bitter thoughts.

"Devon, you'll pardon me if it's none of my business, but are you and Dom involved then?"

Her hand jerked, sloshing a little of the cappuccino's foam up the side of the cup. She was overreacting, giving Aidan all the wrong ideas for why she was upset.

"I don't mean to pry. It's only…" He set his own cup down carefully before continuing, "I thought there might be something between you and Bennett."

Devon smiled wanly, tucking her hands beneath the table in her lap. Straightening, she took a deep breath and looked directly at Aidan. "Actually, I'm not involved with either one of them." Aidan seemed taken aback. She nodded before continuing, "Dom and I practically grew up together. We've known each other since we were young children and I can promise we've never been anything more than good friends. Best friends, really."

"But—"

"It's complicated. My fault, I made it that way. I'm hurt. He broke a promise to me, one given in good faith. I thought better of him, but he lied. Considering he's like a brother to me, it took me off guard."

Aidan listened, barely moving. When Devon glanced up, he nodded slightly in encouragement.

Weary from being closed off to the people around her, Devon decided to confide for once. After all, what did it really matter? Dominic was part of her inner circle, as much family as her own father. And he'd deceived her, betraying her trust.

She swallowed. "As for Bennett, we were attracted to each other." Devon scanned Aidan's face, seeing only reassurance and acceptance. She continued, shaking her head. "I'm so confused. We're still attracted, I suppose. Yes." She fumbled to a halt, wrinkling her brow. "But everything's gotten in the way. Dominic. Natalie. Our own baggage, maybe."

Devon looked somewhere beyond Aidan and the little café table they shared, thinking of what had been lost with Bennett. "We only lasted a moment, and then it was gone before it fully formed. At the time, I thought we might be more."

Aidan shifted, staring wordlessly into her eyes as she refocused on him. "I'm sorry, Devon. I'm sorry you're sad."

Heat suffused her face. She shouldn't be talking about Bennett this way. And not with Aidan. "No, I'm sorry I'm overly sensitive about Dominic. Sometimes I take things more personally than I should, but I'm being silly."

Aidan paused, continuing to watch her. Devon flashed a quick smile, trying to diffuse the serious mood. He remained intent, finally speaking. "The way I see it, Devon, you have every right to be upset. Your best friend broke his word to you. Now maybe he has an explanation, but it seems to me he could have offered one before now."

Aidan was a wonderful man. He simply didn't understand the nature of liars. It was yet another example of how she was different, destined not to fit with most people.

Average, honest people.

Picking up her cup, she smiled over the rim. "I'm sure he has an explanation, Aidan. But really, it was foolish of me to ask anything of him. Let's not waste any more thought on it."

"Wait," Aidan stopped Devon from changing the subject. "Foolish to ask what you did, or foolish to ask for anything at all?"

She frowned into his patient gaze. "Is there a difference?"

Another man jostled their table, interrupting their conversation. Relieved, Devon smiled broadly at the other customer, reassuring him that she and Aidan were fine, along with their coffees. Switching her smile to Aidan, she stood, signaling the end of their break. As she wrapped her scarf and put on her jacket, she knew she'd never been lonelier, surrounded by a city of strangers.

***

"DEVON!"

Dominic slung his coat over the stairwell post in the entryway before continuing into the flat. Looking first into the kitchen, then dining room, he popped his head around the corner into the sitting room before seeing her. She was settled in the armchair while a small fire flicked its flames at the grate next to her.

"Hey, am I late? I thought we were going to that new place down the road for some blues and dinner? Why aren't you dressed?"

"Dom, I'm perfectly dressed. In fact, I'm quite comfortable where I am." She reached over to the table beside her where he realized she'd poured herself a modest measure of brandy. "Anyway, I thought you might want to take Natalie. It sounds like a nice, romantic sort of place."

She shot him a bland look before tipping the snifter up to her lips. Stepping carefully into the room, he came closer as she swallowed and set the glass down gently, watching him. He'd never known Devon to drink brandy. She could knock back whisky, vodka, or any god-awful concoction with rum, but she couldn't sip even the finest brandy without a shudder wracking through her on the first swallow.

She propped her chin on one hand, waiting him out. Briefly, he considered a wild excuse, some fabrication she might believe. But this was Devon. And it was time she heard the truth.

It never occurred to him she might have deserved it sooner.

"Devvie, I can explain."

"But there's no need, Dominic. I clearly saw for myself today that you're seeing Natalie, so I don't need you to explain it to me."

He sat down slowly, stalling for time to take the full measure of her mood. "I know you're upset. I get that. But please let me explain."

She picked up the glass again, giving it one expert swirl before cupping it between her hands. Sighing, she said, "Dominic, you seem awfully determined. If you insist on my enlightenment, then I'll indulge you. But there's only one thing I want to know."

"What?"

"Did you ever step away from Natalie as I asked? Or has this been going on from the beginning, practically since you got here?"

He dropped his eyes to examine the carpet. "Devvie, you have to listen. You don't understand everything going on. I know it seems like I lied, but—"

Devon sat forward, ash-dark eyes boring into his. "Don't sit there and act like this is a misunderstanding! You *did* lie to me. I want to know if it was outright or by omission." At his blank look, she raged on. "You either deceived me from the outset, with no intention of keeping your word or it was later, when you rekindled this *romance*," she practically sneered the word, "and failed to tell me."

He reached out for her hand, confounded when she snapped back from him.

"Either tell me which it was, or leave me alone. I've no interest in your justifications, Dominic. I have even less interest in any arguments you have that this was necessary or vital to some scheme I've been left out of. *As usual.*"

She spat the words, vibrating with raw energy as she clutched the brandy between hands knuckled white in anger. He'd never seen her so furious, and his chest tightened as he fully comprehended the hurt he'd caused.

Deflated next to her pulsing resentment, Dom sighed.

"Why do you want to know, Dev? Does it matter?"

"Because one scenario suggests you might actually care about her. Maybe you rationalized it to yourself, not seeing any harm since Bennett and I were over. The other suggests you only care about yourself, Dominic, and whatever plans and plots you've cooked up. It's *Machiavellian*." She lowered her voice, practically whispering her pained words. "I'm truly afraid you're the kind of man who sacrificed my trust, and probably Natalie's feelings by now, for something you've told yourself is *more important*. The end justifies the means, right, Dom?"

"Jesus, Devvie, how can you think so little of me?"

She exploded out of the chair, slamming her glass down on the table so hard he was amazed it didn't shatter.

"If you did that, how can *you think so little of me?*"

He stood, more than topping her in height but unable to match her temper. Shaking his head, he looked into the fireplace where the embers now glowed red. "Why is this important? Why are you taking this so damn personally? For God's sake, I've taken the woman out a few times! *Why does it matter, Dev?*"

She stepped back from him, gathering herself. Picking up her brandy, he saw the amber contents shake as she held the glass. Seeing his gaze, she tossed the remainder into the fading fire, staring as the flames shot orange and gold before dying back down. She turned her head to him, and he saw her eyes had returned to palest gray.

"It matters because I needed a favor, Dom. And I've never asked you for *anything*."

***

Ultimately, Devon left the flat soon after Dominic made his silent exit. Her thoughts were too complicated, too dark for the solitary space once the sky had turned to night. The fire died and the soft lamps only accented the inkiness surrounding her. She wanted to be around people.

Even if they were strangers.

After all, did anyone ever really know someone else? After Dominic's latest actions, she wasn't sure.

"Well, hello. Dirty martini, yes?"

She'd migrated to a place she knew, the gastropub. Its familiarity beckoned. She wouldn't admit it also reminded her of Bennett.

The bartender smiled as he quickly wiped down the area in front of her before placing a coaster down. She looked at him blankly before remembering he'd been working the night she and Bennett argued, then left together.

"Yes," she smiled. "A dirty martini is as good a place to start as any, right?"

"It certainly is." He placed the martini in front of her with a nod then walked away to take care of other waiting customers.

Devon tasted her cocktail, finding it flawless. The icy vodka skated down her throat, easing the lingering tightness left over from her confrontation with Dom. She set her glass down, making sure she paced herself. Not one to usually drink, she'd made a bit of a habit of it lately.

A frown creased her forehead.

Alcohol was no fix for what ailed her.

Devon was lonely. Even in the crowded bar, she felt isolated, cut off from the people milling about her. If she were honest, she'd felt this way for a long time, even before she'd come to London.

She'd plunged herself into school and work to be useful to her father. Succeeding beyond anyone's wildest imagination, she'd used academia and her incredible intelligence to wall herself away from people. She couldn't explain her childhood, or herself, to people. So, she'd made sure no one got close enough to ask.

She kept her father and by extension, Dom and his father, very close. She counted on her family to fill the gaps loneliness cut into her, maybe since her mother left without a word so long ago. They understood her.

Or so she'd thought.

She drained her drink, damning herself and Dominic. Alcohol wasn't a solution to anything, but there were times when she could let loose a little. It was time she stopped being so hard on herself, holding herself to standards no one could possibly meet.

At the bartender's raised brow toward her empty glass, she nodded. He fixed another, adding extra olives with a flourish.

She raised her glass to him, distantly noting he seemed a bit blurry. She recalled drinking the hateful brandy earlier, and now vodka besides.

It was probably the lighting. Disregarding any worries, she fished out an olive with one delicate finger and caught the dripping vodka on her tongue. Then she popped it into the air, capturing it between her teeth. Absentmindedly, she chewed and sipped while contemplating the crowd with her chin propped on a fist.

A little later, she caught the bartender's eye, winking at her now empty glass. When had that happened?

He cocked his head, eyeing her as he thrummed his fingers on the bar. "Okay, but let's slow it down a little. Agreed?" He took his time mixing her a fresh martini, this one with more olive juice and less vodka. Devon never noticed.

With a dreamy smile, she started to pat his hand but knocked into the glass instead. He caught the stem, straightening it before it could spill. With a brief hesitation, he pushed a sparkling water in front of her, edging the martini to the side.

"I see you're at it again."

Devon swiveled in her chair to see Bennett standing right behind her. He braced an arm on the bar, effectively caging her in.

The bartender, unsure if the man had been speaking to him or the lady, backed away unnoticed.

"What's it to you, boss?"

A muscle bunched in his jaw. "As I said, you're here again, drinking too many martinis and flirting with the staff. I'd say you're in danger of becoming cliché."

"Cliché would be me throwing this drink in your face. Lucky for you, I don't like to waste good vodka." She waved a careless hand toward her seltzer. "Be warned though; I do have a handy glass of water. I'd hate to spill it on you." She smiled, vaguely amused with her own moxie. Sensing Bennett's impatience, she rose to leave. For both their sakes.

He clamped a hand on her forearm, stopping her. "Where do you think you're going?"

"I'm leaving. I don't want to fight with you. Otherwise, I might add that you're here again too. Did you come with Natalie?"

He threw his head back, bewildered. "No, I didn't. I'm alone. Natalie and I are not seeing each other, Devon. Nor have we ever. Didn't you believe me?"

She sighed, slumping back onto her stool. "Yes, I guess so. But only because she's seeing someone else."

"Dominic."

"Yes."

"Are you upset by that?"

"Yes, but not for reasons you think. There's nothing between Dom and me either," she said. "He's like family."

She stood again, ready to push past him but wobbling a little instead.

Bennett braced a hand to her back in support, amusement creasing his eyes. He didn't budge so much as an inch out of her way.

"Where do you want to go?" He asked as she pushed ineffectually against him.

Frustrated beyond belief, Devon neatly stomped a foot in temper. Unknowingly, she appeared young and crossly cute. Bennett promptly burst out in laughter.

"All right, let's get you home."

She stubbornly planted her feet.

Bennett continued to laugh, all while draping her coat over her shoulders and buttoning her into it. "Devon, please come with me. After all, I'm here because I'm tired of my own company." Her eyes met his, concentrating on his words. "I'm here because it reminds me of you. Of us."

He leaned in and brushed his lips lightly over hers. She looked up at him, weakened. His honesty, coupled with his tenderness, robbed her of any defenses.

"Can we call another truce? Please?" He held out his hand, inviting her to take it.

If he but knew it, she couldn't resist him when he simply asked, rather than demanded. She laced her fingers with his.

Meeting his eyes, she saw desire, mingling with need. He wanted her. And she wanted him, so much.

Why shouldn't she have him, even if it was only for a while?

"Okay, Bennett," she sighed her acceptance of everything his eyes asked. "Truce."

He caught her to him, pressing her up as he angled his mouth over hers in a hard, breathless kiss. Speechless, she could only smile before he looped an arm around her shoulders, leading her out of the pub.

As they stepped on the sidewalk, she looked up at him, clear gray eyes meeting midnight blue.

"Bennett?"

"Yes?"

"Our truce?"

"Yes?"

"Well, it's more of a trial cease fire. So don't get cocky."

She heard him chuckle as they walked into the night, toward his waiting car.

***

Whisper light kisses brushed Devon's face, touching her cheeks before darting to lightly lick the corners of her lips. She opened her mouth, bringing her tongue out to chase the soft intruder, tasting hints of spice and mint he left behind.

Murmuring, she turned her head, seeking solace when a quick nip to her earlobe brought her fully awake.

Drowsily, she opened her eyes to Bennett's, inches away. Looking to the side, she saw they were in his car, where she'd apparently dozed off on the drive to her flat. Bennett's palm on her cheek brought her head back around, bringing him back into her focus.

He dropped his mouth on hers, demanding everything she could give.

She sparked into flames. Desperate to be closer, she fumbled with her seatbelt until he reached down and deftly released it. Reaching behind her, he pulled her closer. Their tongues and hands danced and explored, breaking only for hurried gasps before pressing close again. She was scarcely aware he'd unbuttoned her coat until she felt his cool hands slip beneath her blouse to brush her abdomen. Sucking in a breath, she loosed a husky laugh, lost in the rapture of being with Bennett after so long without him.

"Somehow you fit me perfectly. Touch me more." She smiled up through long lashes while starting to unfasten his coat.

He quickly took advantage of her exposed neck, grazing the skin with his teeth before soothing it with soft licks and pressed kisses. When he reached her ear, he rubbed his cheek closer, whispering, "I knew we'd fit since the first time I laid eyes on you, Devon. Even after you broke my nose."

She gurgled with laughter, thumping him so he would lean back. Lowering her eyes, she concentrated on unbuttoning his coat and spreading it open. She ran her hands over his chest, letting her right palm rest over his heart, feeling its rapid beat.

She lifted stormy gray eyes to his, preserving a moment she'd remember all her life. "Make love with me, Bennett."

He rested his forehead on hers, as if waiting to see if she would change her mind. After a few seconds, he raised his head to press a kiss to her forehead. Lifting the hand she'd placed over his heart, he pressed it to his lips in a reverent kiss.

"Yes."

CHAPTER ELEVEN

"I'M PERFECTLY ABLE TO WALK, you know." Devon laughed as Bennett carried her to her door.

He crouched slightly so she could fit her key into the lock. "Uh uh. I'm not letting go now that I have you where I want you. Besides, I'm not so certain you *can* walk. You had quite a buzz going back there."

"I'm perfectly capable of walking. But I'll let you carry me since you're so good at it." She grinned cheekily as he elbowed through the door and shut it with his shoulder.

"Which way?"

She knew he was giving her the chance to change her mind. With no intention of doing so, she waved a hand, signaling the way. "All the way back and to the left."

He leaned down for a brief but devastating kiss before heading down the hallway and opening the door to her bedroom. Laying her down on the bed, he leaned over her in apparent consideration.

Uncomfortable with his hesitation, she reached up and grabbed his lapels. Tugging hard, she toppled him down onto her where she claimed his mouth just as he opened it in protest. When he moved to push himself up, Devon jerked his coat down over his shoulders, effectively trapping his arms. She kissed his face, administering a playful nip when she reached his jawline.

Bennett groaned, capitulating. Fighting with the sleeves of his coat, he rolled to his side.

Devon immediately pushed him to his back, climbed astride and started unbuttoning his shirt. Bennett managed to free his hands and reach for hers as she bent her head, nuzzling his bare chest before finding one flat nipple and tonguing it in erotic whorls.

She raked her nails lightly over his other nipple before grazing his abdomen. Bennett's erection strained, bulging between them, and she grasped its length before taking both hands to the task of his belt.

She was a vortex of energy, swirling over him. Bennett reached up to push off her coat. Hurriedly grasping her blouse, he pulled it over her head. As she loosened his belt and went to work on his trousers, he sat up and suckled her breast through the lacy fabric of her bra. Belatedly, he impatiently shrugged off his coat and shirt.

Once free, he reached around to remove her bra, cupping her breast while thumbing the nipple in a rough rhythm. He latched his lips onto the other, forming a hard suction with the roof of his mouth while alternately soothing it with the flat of his tongue.

Devon groaned, throwing her head back and flooding with warmth. She clasped his head, trying to ease the tension he provoked in her. But Bennett only sucked harder and plucked her other nipple between thumb and forefinger.

"Bennett, *please*."

His lips curved against her. Looking down, she caught the erotic vision of his dark head at her breast. She ran her fingers through his thick hair, tousling it before tugging him back. As he lifted his head, dark blue eyes drowsy with passion met hers. Lowering her hand, she fully unzipped him.

She gripped his shaft, lightly running her finger over the moist tip.

Groaning, Bennett murmured, "Devon, no, I'm too close."

She gently squeezed before lowering her mouth to taste the smooth crown of him, lightly licking before closing her lips around the broad head of his penis. Bennett abruptly flipped her onto her back, crouching above her. He went to work on her pants, unzipping and pulling them down in one long motion before crawling back up the bed. He propped himself above her, framing her face between his palms.

They kissed, long and slow. There was an underlying desperation in Devon, knowing how fleeting and fragile their truce might be. Unable to bear the thought of losing him, she locked her gaze on his. His eyes were feral, intensely exhilarating and breathtaking.

He kissed her neck, moving down to brush along her collarbone to her breast. Scraping his stubble over the sensitive peaks, he continued downward. Her abdomen quivered as he blew lightly, cooling her overheated skin before rimming her bellybutton with the tip of his tongue. She sucked in a breath, hollowing out her stomach as desire washed over her in heated waves.

She spread her legs, inviting him to press his engorged erection to her core. But he resisted, kneeling back onto his knees so he could grip her hips and pull them up onto his thighs.

Devon gasped, feeling exposed even though she still wore her panties. She reached, trying to bring him back to her, needing the reassurance of his bulk. Bennett captured her hands and trapped them beneath his own against her breasts, moving in small circles so she rubbed her own flesh. Taking her index finger, he brushed it over her nipple, pebbling it to painful hardness.

She caught her breath, moaning, surprised at the unexpected pleasure he created with her own hands. Her eyes closed in pleasure as he circled and pressed, then squeezed with her hands caught beneath his own. She ran her tongue over her lips to moisten them, opening her eyes as he let out a groan of his own.

He stared at her mouth with wild concentration, his jaw tense. He took a deep breath, nostrils flaring while he seemed to battle for control. Devon shifted, flexing her hips to accommodate him. Bennett's pupils dilated, nearly consuming the blue into black. Dropping his hands to her hips, he grasped her panties before tearing them neatly into scraps around her.

Shocked, she looked down as he scooped both hands beneath her and pulled her closer before lowering his mouth to her core. She flung an arm up to muffle her scream as he ruthlessly plunged his tongue into her moistness. She panted, unable to catch her breath. Arching her back, she squirmed in an agony of wanting. Nearing her peak, she restlessly clawed the sheets, unsure if she wanted to cling or pull away. Suddenly, Bennett gentled, soothing her with his tongue, licking up her slit to find her aching nub.

She whimpered, unable to tolerate his acute attentions, trying to wriggle away as the pleasure built.

"Bennett," she gasped, "please, no. I can't."

He continued to lick in soft circles, delicately. "You can, Devon." He flattened his tongue on her, pressing gently. "You will." With that, he closed his lips on her and sucked hard as she splintered all around him, shaking and crying out as the orgasm wracked her.

Her breathing slowed to find Bennett braced over her, lightly kissing her closed eyelids. She blinked them open to see his eyes were a brilliant blue, brighter than she'd ever seen. Devon smiled, cherishing the intimate knowledge. She catalogued and cradled the differences in him as they made love, harboring her lover's secrets.

He drew a finger down her cheek, caressing the soft skin before running it over her lower lip. "You okay?" He whispered, barely stirring the quiet cocoon they shared. A dim light cast shadows over them, enhancing their solitude.

She stretched, catching his erection between her folds as she rubbed sinuously against him. "I'm fine. How are you?" She caught his finger between her teeth, holding it while she tasted its tip. Smiling around his finger, she teased him with a light suck before pushing it out.

Bennett leaned down and kissed her, hard, chasing her tongue before dueling with it in a sexual dance. In response, she raked her hands down his back, grasping to pull him harder into her.

He thrust against her slick folds, mimicking the sex act. She moaned, instantly aroused again, but wanting more.

"Bennett, I want you. Inside me."

She angled her pelvis and caught the tip of his shaft inside her. Bennett froze, sweat beading on his forehead. With eyes tightly closed, he braced his arms in corded strain.

"Goddammit, Devon, stay *still.*"

She brushed a lock of hair back from his forehead, enjoying his fine tremor as she touched his sweat soaked skin. "I can't, Bennett." As she repeated his earlier words, his eyes flew open to meet the ebony rimmed gray of hers. "I won't." She flexed, inviting him further into her while pressing a palm to his low back.

Bennett threw back his head, growling as he surged into her. With both hands beneath her hips, he arched her into him while rearing back to nearly pull out before thrusting back inside her, over and again. He couldn't seem to get close enough, and paused just long enough to lift her legs higher around his waist and grab a pillow to prop beneath her bottom. Starkly intent, he resumed his powerful pace.

Devon sobbed, biting into her arm to keep from crying out in wild abandon. She was so close, each thrust rubbing his pelvic bone against her in tortuous pleasure. She arched her back, trying to satisfy the ache, and Bennett instantly responded, sensing what was needed. Shifting to brace himself on one arm, he continued to drive into her while pressing his thumb over the sensitized bundle of nerves throbbing for him.

The orgasm ripped through her, causing her to rhythmically clench and unclench around Bennett's steely length. He hardened further, arching his back and giving her nub one last chafing caress that threw her into a second, powerful climax. Her sheath fiercely contracted and he shouted as he reached his own peak, unable to hold back its pulsing force.

He collapsed on her, momentarily too weak to hold himself up any longer. They both took deep, shuddering breaths, hearts racing in tandem. As they quieted and the room cooled around them, Bennett raised his head, looking deep into her eyes.

Suddenly shy, Devon leaned up to take his lips in a breathlessly tender kiss.

***

Bennett wasn't giving Devon any chances to feel awkward. Or worse, regretful.

Grabbing a pillow, he fluffed and propped it behind her shoulders. "I'm running you a bath." She opened her mouth to speak, but he pressed a finger to her lips, silencing whatever she might have said. "So you won't stiffen up."

Her face colored, and she nervously smoothed her hair. Bennett caught her hand and turned its palm upward before pressing a soft kiss on her wrist.

She blushed more fiercely, biting her lip. He rose before she tempted him further. He wanted to charm her, spoil her a little. As he reached the doorway, he looked back, where she sat flushed and flustered. His heart stuttered, and then fell.

She was perfect, everything he'd ever wanted or would want again.

Now he needed to seduce her heart, not just her body.

She was drowsy but still awake when he returned a little while later. Holding a hand out to her, he breathed in relief as she accepted his invitation. She rose, silently holding onto him as he led her to the bath. He'd run a full tub, lit two fat candles on mismatched plates, and poured glasses of a deep, red wine.

She glanced up, inquiring.

"I'm joining you. I'm not giving you time alone so you withdraw from me and isolate yourself." At her startled look of defense, he brushed a curl of her hair over her shoulder. "I'm not criticizing you, Devon. But you close people off, and I want in. *Please*."

She looked back at him, gravely. After a long moment, she nodded. Bennett breathed a silent sigh of relief before tugging the belt of her robe, untying the knot.

She stood tall as the robe dropped to her feet. Admiring her courage, he pulled her toward the bath where she daintily stepped into the foamy water. Bennett was immobilized, captured by her beauty.

"Well? Aren't you coming?" She was smiling at him, seemingly bemused by his attention.

"Yes, I am." He quickly tossed off his trousers and dropped the unbuttoned shirt he'd shrugged on to the floor. He wore nothing else and her eyes quickly dropped to his jutting erection.

Following her glance, he chuckled. "Don't worry. I *can* control myself." He promised himself he would. "Let's get you settled."

She eased down into the warm water, relaxing back against the curved porcelain with her legs stretched out full length to touch the other end. Unmoving, she watched as he knelt beside her. She sighed as he twisted the length of her hair into a messy coil before securing it back with a clip he found on her dressing counter.

"You're quite good at this. A woman might be forgiven for thinking you'd done it before."

Bennett tutted, frowning a little. "You're wrong. Besides, everything is new with you, Devon." Reaching to hand her a glass of wine, he let their fingers brush as she accepted it. After she'd taken a sip, he tenderly tipped her chin until her eyes leapt to his. "I don't want to embarrass you, but we need to talk. It was your first time, and I—"

She put a finger to his lips, silencing him. With a silent shake of her head, she reached forward and picked up his glass. She handed it over before removing her finger, but not before pressing it slightly, as if to seal his lips shut on the conversation he wanted.

Bennett let her have her way, for the moment at least. Tapping his glass against hers, he watched as she brought her glass to her lips before asking, "Don't you want to know what we're toasting?"

"I'm afraid to ask." She started to tip her glass up, but relented at his intent stare. Lowering her glass, she asked, "Okay, have it your way. What are we toasting?"

"Us." He took a long swallow of wine while she gaped at him. Before she could recover, he set his glass down and tunneled one hand into the back of her hair, bringing her to him. He captured her mouth, reclaiming her in a kiss that was both commanding and tender. He thoroughly ravished her before pulling back, satisfied to see stunned pleasure in the dreamy mist of her eyes. "Finally, we have our beginning. *To us.*"

Although she still held it, her glass tipped precariously. He carefully removed it to set it on the rim of the tub. Tracing a finger over her face, he pushed a wayward strand of hair behind her ear.

"Will you answer one question for me?"

She rolled her eyes, playfully. "Yes, what is it?"

"I need to know that you don't regret what just happened between us. You'd been drinking, Devon. I'm afraid that's going to give my conscience some bad moments."

"No, Bennett. NO." She gripped his arm, squeezing to further emphasize her words. "I knew what I was doing, every step, every minute of the way. I need you to *listen* to me."

Caught up in her urgency, he stared into her determined face. "Okay. I am."

"I wanted this. I wanted *you.*" She blushed a little, but firmly went on. "I still do. I admit I'm a little unnerved, maybe even shy, but please don't mistake me. Don't misunderstand me, and please don't underestimate me." She smiled broadly, seemingly pleased by her own admission. "I'm so happy you're my first lover. Don't let that overdeveloped sense of chivalry you have put us at cross-purposes now. I'm not sure I could stand it."

Catching him off guard with her smile, Bennett was staggered by her incredible beauty, inside and out. He'd be damned if she'd have any other lovers after him, fair or not. "You're so lovely," he groaned. "How did I ever stay away?"

Her chin trembled and she dropped her eyes. "I don't want to think about those days," she murmured.

Not wanting to upset or embarrass her, he tapped her knees, signaling her to make some room. As she looked up, he grinned.

"Budge up, woman. Or don't you want to share that bath?"

Bennett slipped behind her, cradling her between his legs as he settled into the warm water. Devon reclined against him, and the familiar tingle of attraction jolted between them. With his heart banging an unsteady tattoo, he vowed to make her happy beyond this night.

She would be his. Always.

***

Across town, Dominic eased himself from Natalie's bed.

Standing silently, he watched the slow rise and fall of her breasts, indicating she slept soundly despite his movements. His gaze washed over her, stopping to admire her lips, red and swollen from his earlier attentions. A slight smile etched the corners of her mouth upwards, and her brow was smooth, flawless in slumber. Edging backward, he saw the chafed skin of her jaw where his whiskers must have rubbed her skin.

He should have been more careful.

Dominic turned away. Rubbing the back of his neck, he sought to ease the knots gathered there.

He'd been careless.

Sleeping with Natalie had never been part of the scheme. He'd planned to wine and dine her, romance her a bit until he got the information he needed. But upon meeting her, he was instantly, rawly attracted. Spending time with her, and lots of it, had been no hardship.

Looking back, he wasn't sure when he'd lost his way.

He liked her, tremendously. She was funny, smart, and hellishly sexy. She could freeze a man, or woman, to the bone with her ice princess act. But with him, she thawed. It turned out she was everything he could want, all wrapped in a gorgeous package.

She stirred, reaching out to the empty space where he'd been. As she settled back into deep sleep, he silently cursed himself, clenching his fists. He'd forgotten the reasons he was with her, lost control. Now, he must have the strength to reclaim his purpose. He would refocus and regain his bearings.

It was time to complete the task he'd come to do.

He crept silently through her flat, looking for the bag where she kept her laptop. Finding it where she'd dropped it near the doorway, he picked it up and carried it to the furthest bedroom, quietly easing the door shut. He couldn't chance turning on a light, so he worked by the glow of a penlight. Turning on her system, Dom quickly muted it from making any sound.

He knew her password. Unaware of his ulterior motives, she'd let him lean over her as she worked, enjoying his outrageous flirtation. While he'd nuzzled her ear and kissed along her nape, he'd watched as she tapped it out.

It really had been quite simple.

He squeezed his eyes shut, not liking himself much. Wincing, he reminded himself, again, why he was there.

Working rapidly, his fingers flew over her keyboard with the long experience of someone well used to technology. He glanced up periodically, checking to ensure his absence was still unnoticed.

About an hour later, he gently shut her computer, pocketing the flash drive he'd used to download the information. He'd found it all, everything he'd possibly want later. He should have been relieved.

Carefully placing the laptop back into her bag, he then retraced his steps to put it back beside the door. He double-checked that everything looked exactly as it had before, knowing he couldn't be too cautious or attentive to detail.

Slipping his phone out of his back pocket, he sent his father a text.

I'm in.

Dominic paused by the door. Leaving would be the right thing to do, the noblest action he could take for the woman sleeping off their lovemaking. He knuckled his fist against the wall, resting his forehead on it as desire and regret waged a bitter war inside him.

Desire won.

He was back in Natalie's bed, undressed and beneath the covers as she stirred to reach for him again.

CHAPTER TWELVE

IT WAS NEARLY TWO WEEKS before Dom attempted to patch things up with Devon. She had a temper that burned slow, but once she erupted, as she had with him, she always needed time to cool off.

The least he could do was give her that time, considering how hurt she'd been. Dominic ignored the internal whisper that suggested he was avoiding her, consideration be damned.

Guilt and regret dominated his thoughts. He wondered whether the cost of the scheme he and his father had hatched would be too high.

He walked up to Devon's flat, spare key in hand.

Since their argument, he'd spent his nights with Natalie. He condemned himself to hell, but couldn't stay away. Until the day of reckoning came, he took it all, every moment and memory he could make with her.

The lights were on in Devon's flat and he sent up a silent prayer she would be alone. He needed to get back to the States, but wanted to fix things with her first. She was family, and he couldn't stand the idea she was disappointed in him, wounded by his actions.

He unlocked her door, poking his head inside to call out softly. "Dev? Are you home?"

She raced toward him, swallowing him in a hug. He relaxed in her hold; he should have realized she'd want to resolve their differences as much as he. They'd never gone more than a week being mad at each other.

"Dom, you're back. I'm sorry I was so hard on you." She cupped his shoulders between her hands, a soft smile on her face.

Hoarsely, he said, "Devvie, tell me you forgive me."

Embracing him, she bussed his cheek with a quick kiss.

"Of course, Dom. Always. I could never stay angry with you, you know that."

"So we're okay?" He had to ask, needing the reassurance. As family, she meant the world to him. He'd never worried about losing her affection or respect until now.

"Yes, Dom. We're okay. I overreacted, not considering how you felt about Natalie." With a secret smile, she added, "I think I understand better now."

Frowning, he eyed her. Something was different. "What do you mean?"

She patted him. "I've grown up a bit in the past weeks, that's all. And I recognize the signs now, as I'm pretty guilty of most of them myself." At his questioning look, she explained, "You're smitten. It's rather endearing, actually. Especially since it's obvious Natalie's equally taken with you." She turned, leading him into the sitting room.

Dominic followed, zeroing in on the first part of what she'd said. "Wait a minute. Putting Natalie and me aside for a minute, what are you saying about yourself?" At her raised brow, he echoed her earlier comment, "You being *pretty guilty yourself?*"

She chuckled. "While you've been with Natalie, I've spent my time with Bennett." Gesturing him to the sofa, she sat beside him. "There's no need to look panicked. We're happy. *I'm happy*, Dom. I've never felt this way about anyone."

He bit back a groan as she patted his leg, describing how she had him to thank, really.

"It was seeing you and Natalie. We both realized you two were together. And somehow the barriers keeping Bennett and me apart melted away."

Dom turned, facing her while grasping her hand firmly in his. His worst nightmare had occurred; she was serious about Bennett. This was a disaster.

"Listen to me, Devvie. You need to be careful. Don't go soft on me now. You've worked for years to be where you are. Don't throw it away on some fling with your boss."

"This isn't a *fling*, Dominic. I think I'm in love with him." She seemed surprised by her own declaration, then a dreamy smile drifted over her face.

Squeezing her hand, he desperately interrupted her. "No, no, no. Don't do this, Devvie. You don't understand men."

She peered at him, serious. "What do you mean?"

This was the worst scenario. He inwardly cursed himself for leaving her alone while he enjoyed Natalie. "You need to slow down. Whatever you do, don't repeat those words to Bennett." She tugged her hand in his grip. Holding on fiercely, he said, "Are you hearing me?"

"I'm not ashamed of my emotions, Dom. Frankly, I shouldn't have said anything to you before I shared my feelings with Bennett."

Dominic's gut clenched. He couldn't tell her about his plan with their fathers; she'd only interrupt it, possibly ruin everything. But if he didn't warn her away from Bennett, her pain would be inevitable. Pitilessly, he exploited her fears. "You're forgetting where we come from. Do you honestly think Bennett will accept us, our family? Do you think he'll accept *you* when you tell him who you are, and what you've done?"

She paled, but he steeled himself from reassuring her.

"You always said I worried too much. That I shouldn't be ashamed of myself or my family, the cons we played."

"That was before I knew you'd get serious with Bennett Sterling." Her eyes were watery pools of misty gray. "Dammit, Devon. I don't want to see you hurt."

She nodded, obviously lost in her own thoughts. "I'll think about it. But I don't see how Bennett would hurt me, Dom. And I'm happy for now."

Dominic relented. Her vulnerability was palpable and he didn't have it in him to press her further. Besides, he didn't want to risk angering her again. "Okay, I'll leave you be. But be careful, okay?" He didn't wait for her response. "Will you at least trust me for a little advice? I am a man, after all." This time he paused until she reluctantly nodded, a tiny smile lifting the corners of her mouth.

"Don't be a sure thing. Not for him, but especially not for you. Can you hold back a little?"

Devon pondered his question, her forehead creasing slightly. "Fine. But you're going to find out your worries are unfounded. I may lack your experience, but I know what I know."

The woman was stubborn, always had been. He changed the subject. "Okay. For now, let's talk about something else. I'm heading back to the States. Any messages for your dad or mine?"

Surprised, she sprang up. "When are you leaving? Why didn't you say anything sooner?" She wrung her hands, pacing. "Now we've wasted your last two weeks here," she wailed.

"Devvie." She ignored him, striding back and forth. Loudly, he repeated himself. "*Devon.*"

She stopped, facing him.

"I'm coming back. I have something to take care of, in person. I leave later tonight. But after, I'm returning straight away to London."

She whooped. "Oh good. I have so much more to show you."

Dominic rubbed his neck, easing the chronic knots.

Devon saw, misunderstood. Flushing, she rushed into speech. "Oh… *oh.* You're coming back for Natalie. *Of course.*" She immediately beamed down at him. "That's great. Really, that's wonderful, Dom. And I'll still get to see you too. Maybe you'll move some operations for your company here, hey?"

Dominic grimaced, which Devon mistook for embarrassment.

"Never mind. I'll go grab some things I want you to take back to Dad." She rushed from the room.

Dominic stretched, rotating his neck and shoulders. He wanted to tell Devon what he was doing here, but couldn't. Not yet. Now his timing would be critical. He would have to talk to her right away when he returned. After he'd completed the final steps in his project — but before Bennett found out and the backlash swamped her.

He scrubbed a hand over his face, pinching the bridge of his nose. It would be a gamble whether Devon emerged from his actions professionally unscathed. It had always been a known risk; one he and both their fathers decided was acceptable. Dominic had placed his bets on her, confident her abilities would salvage her career.

But that was before the Bennett complication.

With a heavy sigh, Dominic slumped against the couch. Never had he anticipated so many problems with what seemed to be a perfect plan.

Natalie was another unintended casualty.

Although they'd been casual, even lighthearted in their flirtation, the boundaries had quickly blurred. Only he'd known of known his purpose in seeking her out, pursuing a relationship. She certainly hadn't. He was certain she trusted the pleasure they shared at face value with no suspicion of ulterior motives on his part.

Dominic huffed out a bitter laugh.

The playing field was decidedly uneven between them, something he'd avoided in all the cons over all the years. Until now.

Natalie was collateral damage.

As Devon would be, inevitably.

Dominic rubbed at his chest, taking a pained breath.

He was a liar. Telling lies on top of lies.

He'd be glad when this damn job was finished.

***

"Maybe someday you'll tell me why you seem obsessed with these places." Bennett joked as he and Devon walked through the City of London Cemetery. "Normally, I come here alone, or with Granddad. You have a warped sense of what a date is."

Devon laughed, recounting her other visits to other gravesite locations in London. "I love them. But you'll never get the reasons why out of me." Normally, she would have felt awkward, or at least sad from his questions. But being with Bennett made all that go away.

Maybe someday she *would* share her story of how she developed a love for cemeteries. But not today. Today, she lived for the present, hoarding every moment with him in secret stashes of joy.

"Tell me instead why you come here, and fairly often from the sound of it."

He brought her hand to his lips. "For my grandmother. I visit her grave, especially in autumn and winter. I bring her these." He waved the mass of white roses he clutched in his fist.

She squeezed his hand in sympathy. "That's lovely, Bennett. Why particularly fall and winter?"

"Granddad and I planted rosebushes all around her grave. But they only bloom in spring and summer. So, the rest of the time, we bring bouquets."

"You both must have loved her very much." Devon was taken aback by the wealth of emotion in Bennett's voice. His grandmother must have been some woman to inspire such devotion, even beyond death.

"We did. We still *do*. Our admiration for her didn't stop when she passed away." He strolled along, taking a path that bent to the left. "She had a pure heart with a true spirit. She helped people all her life, never harmed a soul."

Devon choked back the declaration of love hovering on her lips. Doubt assailed her. Remembering her mantra from months ago, she quailed.

I can never have Bennett Sterling.

Could he, *would* he understand her past? If he knew, would he still want her?

Arriving at his grandmother's grave interrupted Devon's dark worries.

ROSE BENNETT STERLING
Love Everlasting
1933 – 2004

The headstone was simple yet stately, dark granite rising up from the masses of rose bushes planted all around it. Even in winter, when nothing was in bloom, it had a striking grace.

"What color are they?" At Bennett's arched brow, she clarified. "The rose bushes. What color are they?"

"White. All white. It's the color Granddad and I associate the most with her."

White, the color of purity.

She could imagine them in bloom, easily. They'd be stunning with their dark foliage alongside the stark gray of the marble.

"You were named after her," she said.

"Yes, I was. It's an honor. I miss her very much."

Devon reached up to touch her lips to his cheek. Bennett was an honorable man, capable of deep tenderness. A heavy dullness ached in her chest.

She wished she could be different, somehow.

He must have sensed her disquiet. Placing his palm against her face, he stared into her eyes. "Thank you for coming with me."

She turned her lips into his hand, kissing him. "It's an honor. I wish I could have known her." She linked her fingers with his, silently honoring the woman his grandmother had been.

He bent to lay the bouquet of white roses on her grave. Holding her hand, he gazed down thoughtfully before raising his eyes back to Devon's.

"You weaken me." Taking her unaware, he went on. "You're so perfect, inside and out. You take my breath away."

"No, Bennett." His brows lowered in confusion. Devon continued, "I'm only a woman. Not perfect, not nearly so. I have no need for pedestals."

He shook his head, but said nothing more. After a long moment, he pulled her back down the path they'd come from.

"It's time to go. As much as you love these places, it's time to remember that life is for the living."

He seemed in no rush, though, as they ambled through the park, stopping to comment on particular sculptures or garden elements. They spoke in hushed tones, neither wanting to disturb the peaceful aura of the place.

Once they were buckled into the car, Devon relaxed back into the seat, releasing a long breath. For once, she was glad to leave. The fears and uncertainties she'd suffered moments ago slipped away as happiness snaked its way back into her. Lolling her head, she looked over to the man responsible.

"Ready?" Bennett asked.

"Sure. But what am I agreeing to, exactly?" She smiled lazily, too content for any real concerns.

"Well, we have a train to catch. But first, let's go get your bag."

He wheeled the car around in a U-turn, eyes crinkled with suppressed excitement. She knew better than to ask details. He was hatching a surprise, and she was ready to enjoy it.

He smiled broadly. "Trust me."

***

Devon stared at the rich cream and chocolate brown lacquered paint of the train coach in front of her. An attendant stood in formal livery beside it, assisting with boarding. She watched as Bennett presented their tickets, encased in embossed leather wallets. He insisted on carrying everything, the tickets as well as the luggage they had picked up after leaving the cemetery.

Her things were packed into a brand new rolling hard case, small enough to easily manage but large enough to make her wonder what it contained. He carried his own things in a leather duffel carelessly tossed over one shoulder. Everything had been waiting for them at his townhouse, packed and sitting next to the door.

Of course, Devon questioned everything.

Where were they going?

It's a surprise.

How had he gotten into her flat to have her clothes packed?

I didn't. I picked out new ones at Harrod's and had them sort it.

That had given her pause.

How do you know my sizes?

I've noticed everything about you, Devon.

His face, along with his answer, effectively robbed her of further thoughts or questions. She'd relaxed, deciding to enjoy whatever came.

Now, stunned, she stared at the vintage Pullman waiting to take them away. It was gorgeous, just like the man beside her. Unbeknownst, she looked up at him with her heart in her eyes.

Bennett pulled her to him for a hard kiss that left her wanting and aching for more. He released her, leaving her breathing hard.

"Stop distracting me, woman." He grinned, excitement firing his eyes to a brilliant blue. "Come with me." He led her aboard a coach car while an assistant took their luggage to be stored.

Devon gazed in open-mouthed wonder, amazed at the ornate splendor of the timeless train. The walls were paneled in wood with intricate inlays. Elegant carpet covered the floor of the coach in rich patterns that were echoed in the fabrics covering the armchairs designed as comfortable seating. Sumptuous velvets vied with satiny jacquards. Tables were laid with snow-white linens and delicate china. Crystal and silver reflected in the sunlight shimmering through the cased windows.

"Hmm. I do believe I've managed to surprise you."

Devon turned at Bennett's words, still gaping at her surroundings as she tried to take it all in without missing anything. She heard a muffled chuckle from Bennett before he touched her waist, gently prodding her to advance. He guided her all the way back to the end of the car. The corner was intimate, isolated since the two seats normally across from it had been removed. And unlike any of the others, their table was set with a lush bouquet stuffed with pink peonies. Champagne chilled in a bucket alongside the table, and two flutes waited nearby to be filled.

"Peonies," she sighed. "I love peonies."

"I know." At her questioning look, Bennett explained. "You bought bouquets for your desk all summer long from the market stalls."

"However did you find them in autumn? They must have cost a fortune." She wrinkled her brow.

"Devon," he tipped her chin up so she would look at him. "I would do anything to please you. Don't you understand that yet?"

She wasn't sure she did. Bennett's eyes conveyed a message she was afraid to believe in. She stared, unable to process it.

Taking her clutch purse, Bennett laid it down on the chair, then turned her so he could unbutton her coat. After slipping it down her arms, he handed it with his own to the waiting attendant. Bennett shook his head, waving off another employee as they approached to assist.

Instead, he pulled out her chair himself, prompting her with another touch to be seated. His mouth quirked with amusement. He seemed to enjoy the rare moment of catching her off guard. Pouring their champagne, he pushed a flute closer to her hand that rested limply on the tablecloth.

He waited several long minutes.

"Devon."

She raised dazed eyes to his, questioning.

"I'm crazy about you."

She continued to stare, blankly.

It didn't seem to bother him that she remained silent. "Nothing to say to that?"

She cleared her throat. "Where are we going?" She began looking all around again, oblivious to Bennett's grin.

"Devon."

Her gaze swiveled back to his. "Yes?"

"No, that's where we're going. Devon. Don't you think it's time you visited the place you're named after?"

It was completely perfect. He was everything she'd ever wanted, would *ever* want. She leaned across the table to plant a smacking kiss on him, before subtly deepening it into something more.

As she pulled back, it was Bennett's turn to be surprised, robbed of words.

God, she loved him. She would love him for the rest of her days. With that knowledge, she could take her time. Go at his pace.

With a secret smile, she met his eyes. "Bennett, I'm crazy about you too."

***

He was more than crazy for her. For the first time in his life, Bennett was deeply, madly in love. Olivia was a pale and distant memory, just someone he'd met when he was too young to know the real thing.

He needed to say the words. And yet, there were times when she was mantled in reserve, hesitant with him. It had made him wary of her. While disconcerting, he could admit to himself he'd been suspicious, somehow distrustful of her. Olivia might be firmly in the past, but her effects were lasting.

It was past time to let that go. Trust again. And he would take that leap of faith with Devon. Who better to catch him? She would never disappoint him the way Olivia had. Of that, he was certain.

He must tell her. Articulate the feelings he knew, without doubt, she returned.

All he needed was the perfect moment.

He was brought out of his thoughts as they arrived in Exmouth. It had been a simple thing to jump onto a connecting train from Exeter. And while it didn't possess the luxury and history of the Pullman, they barely noticed. They'd continued to drink champagne during the gourmet three-course lunch that was served earlier.

Nothing could dim their spirits, not even the storm bucketing down outside. Arriving at the hotel in a flurry of laughter, they jostled to stay dry as the heavens unleashed sheets of rain upon them.

Standing under the canopy of the entrance, Bennett shook his head in a spray of droplets. Laughing, he declared, "The one thing I forgot was rain gear."

Devon twisted her hair into a rope to wring it out. Looking up through lowered lashes, she blatantly flirted with him. "Well, I suppose we'll have to figure out something to do inside. It's unfortunate, but I guess we can make do."

He reached for her as she ducked into the revolving door, leaving her luggage behind for him to handle. Allowing the porter to take their bags, he looked at her through the glass. She tossed him a saucy wink then blew a kiss.

He walked through the door, chuckling. She thought she was safe with a glass panel between them.

As he joined her to follow the porter, he leaned down as if to whisper something in her ear. As he felt her relax against him, he snaked his tongue around her earlobe, biting the flesh softly.

He heard her quick intake of breath, before she met his gaze with heavy-lidded eyes.

They rode the elevator silently, each straining toward the other, but trying to maintain some modicum of dignity. The friendly employee wheeling the cart with their bags regaled them with the history of the luxe boutique hotel they were staying in as well as sightseeing tips for the local area.

Bennett shifted to run a tantalizing finger down the slim curve of her spine. She stiffened as he inched his finger around her waist to trace her ribs before lightly caressing the underside of her breast.

Devon clamped her arm down on his hand, trapping it so he couldn't move any further. He splayed his fingers instead, squeezing the soft flesh before darkly chuckling at her stuttered attempts to carry on the conversation with the bellman.

He pulled free as they reached their floor. Tipping the gentleman heavily, he took possession of their bags and key card before the porter could open the room. As soon as the other man cleared the hallway, he pinned Devon against the door, plundering her mouth while hiking one hand to fumble the lock open.

She moaned, lost to everything until a door closed down the hallway.

A discreet cough had Bennett turning his head slightly while still resting his lips on Devon's. A young man stared back, until something in Bennett's gaze had him hurriedly turning away.

The door gave way and Bennett bundled her up to deposit her on the bed. He crawled over her as they both laughed at the other man's expression.

She reached up to tug on his hair. "You lecher. I can't imagine what that poor man thought!"

"He's somewhere wishing he was me. Now shut up and kiss me."

She did. The storm raged outside while they made love, fast then slowly, hard then tenderly, never tiring until the early hours. Late in the morning, they wandered out for a walk, only to hurry back again, fumbling in their eagerness to be together.

They never saw any of the sights the porter talked about.

Bennett cherished her, with his body and soul. Anyone with eyes could see how deeply he loved Devon.

But he never said the words.

CHAPTER THIRTEEN

BENNETT AND DEVON STEPPED OFF the train, arms loosely wrapped around each other. Sorry to see the weekend end, Bennett clasped her to him. As his lips met hers, he tunneled a large hand into her chic chignon, scattering pins around them.

When someone delicately cleared their throat near them, he peered up with heavy eyes.

Natalie met his gaze, one finely arched blonde brow cocked.

"Natalie," he said. "What are you doing here?" Even though she knew his schedule, she rarely appeared unexpectedly during his personal time. He brought Devon close to his side with one arm, aware she was trying to step slightly aside, shielding herself from view.

"Bennett, I do hate to interrupt," Natalie stated blandly. "But I'm afraid I have urgent news. I couldn't get through to you on your phone and, unfortunately, it couldn't wait."

He frowned, knowing the issue must be important for her to come meet him like this. He took few vacations and when he did, Natalie handled things with competent efficiency. In fact, he couldn't recall a problem she hadn't fielded personally, usually briefing him of the pertinent details after the event.

They all walked together, Natalie patiently waiting as Bennett retrieved the luggage.

Bennett turned to Natalie. "Did you drive yourself or take a taxi to get here?"

"I took a taxi, so we could talk on the way back to the office."

With that, Bennett realized the weekend was well and truly over. Natalie was seriously worried, and he trusted her enough to follow her lead.

He frowned, his eyebrows gathering. But Devon patted his arm in reassurance.

"You two need to catch up. Don't worry, I'll grab a taxi to save time."

Bennett hesitated, unwilling to end what had been a perfect idyll.

Natalie intervened. "I really *am* sorry to interrupt," she clasped her hands together, wrinkling her brow. "But I think that would be best. This matter cannot wait, Bennett. And it requires a certain *privacy*, if you understand."

"*Natalie.*" Surely she knew he trusted Devon. Explicitly.

Devon flexed the hand she'd left on his arm, halting his objection. "I understand. Go take care of business. I'll see you later."

He lightly kissed her forehead before ensuring she had a taxi and settling her into it. When he returned to Natalie's side, she stared at him, shaking her head in wonder.

"What?"

"Nothing. Now I see why I never stood a chance, that's all."

Bennett looked at her, horrified.

Natalie laughed. "No worries, Bennett. I'm great, as it turns out. Happy." Smiling at his obvious relief, she continued. "All's well that ends well, yes?"

***

Devon didn't see Bennett again that day. Another day passed, and then a third. He remained embroiled in whatever trauma was shaking the foundations of Sterling International. No one knew what was happening, the hushed whispers through closed meeting room doors telling no one anything.

Not even Devon.

Bennett called, but they were rushed conversations inevitably interrupted by other callers or Natalie. He was in non-stop meetings, new ones being scheduled on top of others. When he couldn't call, he texted, and Devon responded by being comforting, undemanding.

She knew how to do this, to soothe and strengthen without burden. She missed him, horribly. But she fell into old habits of placation, not wanting to drive him away with neediness or by asking too much.

So she waited.

She accomplished a tremendous quantity of work. Even Aidan, when he wasn't looking harassed these days, praised her output. She wondered if he knew what was happening, or whether it was simply pre-wedding nervousness. She'd ask him later when she had the chance.

At the end of the third day, she went home, knowing it would be another evening alone. She checked her watch.

"Dad." She paused, listening as her father fumbled his phone.

After a momentary hesitation, he answered. "Devon, how are you, honey? It's so good to hear from you."

She heard him moving about, and the rustling of papers.

"Is this a bad time?"

Another lull, then, "No, no, not at all. What's happening over there?" His voice pitched slightly higher than usual.

Devon stared at her phone. Telling herself she was imagining problems where there weren't any, she carried on. "I miss you, Dad." She hadn't meant to blurt that out and waited for his usual concerned overreaction.

It didn't come.

In a curiously flat voice, he answered,"I miss you too." That was it.

"Dad, is something wrong?"

Another delay. "No, no. Everything is great."

She heard him draw a deep breath.

Before she could ask anything more, he said, "Tell me about work. How's it going?"

Her normal reticence disappeared. It was her father, after all, and she could share with him. She fully trusted him, even with delicate news.

"Actually, right now there's some kind of emergency. Everyone's on edge, but it's all very hush-hush, and very few people are involved." And she wasn't one of them. "It's probably something global, something with the markets. Or maybe stocks." She hoped it was external. Bennett and his grandfather had worked so hard to build their company. "It'll die down soon, I'm certain."

After a hitch, when she thought she heard papers being shuffled again, he answered. "I'm sure it'll be fine, Devon. Nothing for you to worry about."

Devon was irritated. "Well, let's hope." She hated being patronized. How could he know things would be all right? "Listen, you're distracted, obviously busy. I'll talk to you soon, okay?"

John Sinclair didn't argue. Instead, he told his daughter he loved her and ended the call.

Devon stared at the phone in her hand. That was odd.

But her thoughts quickly returned to Bennett, and all he might be doing. She hoped he would surprise her soon by coming to stay the night. It would be up to him, as she didn't want to show up at a bad time, stressing him further.

No, she would continue to wait. He would come to her.

**

Dominic and Patrick Martin sat across from John Sinclair at his dining room table, drinking espressos as they struggled to understand his side of the conversation with Devon. Finally, John pulled a tablet over and scribbled notes while trying to keep up with what his daughter was saying. He flipped the tablet around so they could read.

Crisis at Sterling.
Still private. No one's talking.
Devon doesn't know.

Patrick looked at Dom, dipping his head towards the doorway. Dominic got up, following him into the kitchen.

Patrick didn't mince words. "She'll know soon. She knows us, and she sure as hell knows you."

Dominic nodded, feeling his gut knot around the slow burn he'd felt since leaving London.

Patrick squeezed his shoulder. "It's time. Go back and finish this."

**

Devon rotated her neck, trying to work out the tension knotting its way into her shoulders. As much as she tried, she couldn't get the numbers in the report she was working on to make any sense. Something was very wrong.

Her phone rang, interrupting the dead silence. Picking up the extension, she answered while applying filters to the spreadsheet, eager to find what must be an error from data entry. She'd double-checked the formulas for accuracy, so that wasn't the problem. But there was a serious anomaly somewhere, as results couldn't change so radically from a week before with only slight market changes.

"*Devon.*"

Aidan's exasperated voice penetrated her concentration. Belatedly, she remembered the phone pressed to her ear.

"Yes, yes, I'm here," she sighed. Maybe she could vent her difficulties to Aidan. "I'm working on this stock valuation report and I can't seem to make any sense of it. Is it possible our files are corrupted?" Pure frustration made her ask, simply because she'd been unable to find the source of the error.

Aidan's voice dropped to a whisper. "*That's why I'm calling you.* Get down here. And don't say anything to anyone, okay? Just save your files, shut down, and come straight to my office." He hung up, not giving Devon time to say another word.

She slowly replaced her phone and did as he asked, wondering what the intrigue was. It wasn't like Aidan to be dramatic, so something was afoot. She paused, thinking. He might need her recent calculations. Shutting and slipping her laptop in a tote bag, she hiked it onto her shoulder. Even if she encountered someone, she doubted she'd raise suspicion.

Clearly, Aidan was getting to her.

She knocked. After cracking the door and shooting a gaze past her to make sure no one was around, he pulled her inside. Devon laid her tote down before sitting across from him, brows raised.

"Aidan, what is going on? You're acting like you've been recruited by MI-5." She laughed, hoping to ease some of the tension, but there was no answering chuckle.

"Keep your voice down, I don't want anyone to know we're here. But, I can't think of anywhere better to go." His eyes moved from side to side, as if he were surveying the area for possible hiding spaces. "Did you bring your laptop? I forgot to ask."

"I did." she said slowly, growing more concerned as his behavior veered from odd to extraordinary. "But why don't you tell me what's going on first."

He leaned in, motioning her to do the same. "Surely you've noticed how uptight Bennett is. Even Natalie is tense about something. They're in full crisis mode." At her nod, he continued. "There's been a security breach. And it's massive."

Devon abruptly sat back, gaping. She swallowed hard before raising a shaking hand to cover her mouth. "Aidan," she croaked, "what's been stolen?"

"Account numbers of our clients. Personal data."

She felt the blood draining out of her face.

Aidan baldly stated the facts. "And money. Loads and loads of money. I suspect that's what you were seeing this morning."

Desperate, she said, "No. Let's go through my reports. It's an error. It must be."

"DEVON," he bellowed.

She started, unused to Aidan raising his voice.

He leaned in again, watching the door to make sure no one came. "Devon," he said in a quieter tone, *"the money is GONE."*

She sat, dazed, while he proceeded to clear space for them to work. He was speaking rapidly, telling her they would start with the corrupted accounts and work backward from there.

She looked up, confused.

"What are we doing, exactly? Aidan, what are we looking for?"

His face was grim. "For the leak. Someone leaked information, and we need to find out who it was."

Devon felt lightheaded. Standing, she went over to his small office refrigerator and took out a bottled water. Taking a long drink, she swallowed and sat back down.

Aidan waited, impatiently. "Okay, power up. We need to get cracking; it's only a matter of time before someone else figures it out."

"But that's okay, right? As long as someone does, and quickly?" At his face, she faltered. "No one else realizes the money has been stolen? *Are you the only one?*"

He sighed, drumming his fingers. "For now. Listen, the worst thing that could happen is if someone discovers the theft and calls the police. Knowing Bennett, and his ethics, he might well do it. If that happens, we may as well declare ourselves incompetent and forfeit the business. *The public mustn't know.*"

"I'm not sure it can be prevented," she cried. "Even finding out who leaked the information, how can we not report what's happened?"

"Finding the person responsible is only the first step. We must get the money *back*. I'm hoping we find something, anything, that creates an opportunity. If we hurry, we'll have the benefit of surprise."

"You think it's an inside job." Her tone was flat, conveying her horror.

"I do. Now power on, and bring your files up."

She busied herself, mind racing with the implications of what she'd heard. Aidan didn't want to involve the authorities, if possible. Relief had her eyes watering before she blinked them clear. An old reflex, but she didn't want the police anywhere near this. A sickness was unraveling in her belly, knowing this was the work of a hacker. A genius with inside knowledge.

Devon knew someone exactly like that.
Dominic Martin.

***

Devon and Aidan worked through the long evening, poring over reports. Aidan's fiancée, Jane, came and went, bringing sandwiches and coffees. She never asked what was happening, just kissed Aidan softly on the cheek before leaving again.

Finally, he heaved a deep breath, pushing himself back from the desk as he stretched.

Devon looked up, eyes bleary. "Did you find something?"

He ignored her, rotating his neck while he looked up at the ceiling. Long moments passed. Then, "Yes."

"*And?*"

"Only a handful of people had access to the kind of data that was accessed and stolen, particularly one aspect of it." He pointed to a report lying on the desk, circling one column with his index finger. "This gave it away, as it required a high level of security."

"Okay." She was impatient. "Who?"

"The only people with access to this particular information are Bennett, Natalie, myself, and…" he paused.

"*Yes?*"

"You. Normally, you wouldn't have, but Bennett must have granted it when you started touring sites with him. Your ID is linked to the pass security."

Devon breathed deep, silent and waiting. The next minutes were critical.

She knew she had nothing to do with this mess, but wasn't sure if he would believe her.

"Do you have anything you want to say, Devon?"

She eyed him straight, never flinching. "Is there something in particular you *need* for me to say, Aidan?" She found herself stressing his name, as if to emphasize their friendship.

"No." He laid his hands on the work table, palm up. His eyes cleared, then his brow smoothed out from where it had been drawn down for hours. "I know I'm not wrong about you." He never broke eye contact. "I trust you."

She laid her hands on his, palm to palm. Letting her breath out, she admitted to herself how much his friendship mattered. Especially now.

"Thank you."

She squeezed, then pulled her hands free.

"I need some time. I have to look into something." She saw his hesitation, and pressed further. "I just need a little time, and a little space."

He sighed, leaning back in his chair. After a long moment, he seemed to come to a decision. "I'll stall as long as I can."

She stood, gathering her things. As she started to collect her laptop, she hesitated, shooting him a questioning look. Would his trust extend to allowing her to remove all they'd worked on that evening?

At his reassurance, she packed it back into the tote bag.

She turned to go. Looking back over her shoulder, she gave a small nod.

Then she disappeared out the door.

***

Natalie looked down at the text, gripping her phone with excitement as she re-read the words.

On my way.
Don't say anything.
Meet me at the airport.
I'll explain then.

Not the most romantic of missives, but she'd take it. It was the content that mattered.

Dominic was on his way back, returning to her. This time, she was determined not to play it so safely. She'd missed him in the weeks since he left, terribly, but never so much as the past few days amid all the strain at work and with Bennett. She'd worked unending hours at Bennett's side, scrambling to provide information as fast as he called for it.

She still didn't know all the details herself. Bennett had flatly refused all requests to tell her exactly what was going on. Maybe, in fairness, he still wasn't sure.

She'd never seen him so obsessed with privacy. They worked in a world where it was necessary, even critical, for complete discretion. But they'd always spoken freely with each other, knowing trust was absolute.

He probably told Devon.

She dismissed the unworthy thought as soon as it formed. Bennett was her past. She was happy now, more than she'd thought possible. Even though her feelings for Dominic had proven to be complicated, she was pleased. He was smart, sexy, and fun. This time around, she'd share her appreciation for him more openly.

She looked up to see the subject of her thoughts walking toward her. He was focused, but seemed to be missing her among the crowd meeting loved ones from the flight. She watched as he looked around, searching.

She walked up to him, unseen. "Hey stranger," she murmured the words near his ear, still unnoticed.

Dom swung his head sharply around. "Hey," his tone oddly hesitant, "what are you doing here?"

He must be jet lagged. She chuckled, holding up her phone with his text message. "I'm here to pick you up. Like you asked, silly." She reached up to kiss him, feeling the brush of his stubble against her face.

There was a pause, and then he pressed his lips to hers. After too short a time, he pulled back, looking away. Hurt flashed through her, making her take a step backwards.

She studied him. His eyes were red-rimmed with fatigue. She raised a hand to his face, sensing a vulnerability previously unseen.

"You're tired. Let me help you." She spoke softly, leading him away.

He was back. That was all that mattered.

***

Dominic allowed Natalie to guide him out of the airport.

He scrubbed his face, rubbing his eyes in an attempt to clear them of the dragging fatigue from too many days with too little sleep.

He recalled sending his text message earlier, as he stood in security at Chicago O'Hare International Airport. He'd been brief, and utterly vague, on purpose. No matter how hard the next hours promised to be, he would face them head-on. With the culmination of his plans, a reckoning awaited.

And he'd meet what was coming face to face.

The timing of his next steps was critical. The information he'd withheld needed to be shared, and at the right moment, or careers could be lost. He refused to think about the emotions of everyone involved.

He could, and would, carry out the final actions as planned. Dominic never left a job unfinished.

But he'd made an unforgivable error.

As he watched the feminine sway of Natalie's hips walking in front of him, he cursed himself viciously.

He'd mistakenly sent the text to Natalie instead of Devon.

***

Bennett carefully hung up the phone. He pressed his knuckles to his forehead, trying to contain the fury bubbling up, but it spilled over as he slammed a clenched fist on his desk. Rage engulfed him as he brought it down again and again, bruising the flesh. A wounded roar escaped, and he spun his chair to look out over London in a wary attempt to find peace.

He closed his eyes, but all he saw was Devon and her lying eyes. They'd laughed and loved, and all the while she'd planned to steal everything she could from him. He vaulted from the chair, pacing. He'd been worried about her innocence when she was little more than a thieving criminal.

She was worse. She'd used him up, bartering with her body to get to the big payday. And he'd fallen for it, every single bit.

Like a fool, he'd anticipated being with her again after the many last, lost days. He hadn't even questioned her silence for the past several hours. No calls. No texts. And now he knew why.

He cursed her while unconsciously rubbing the ache around his heart.

He was damned if she would ruin him.

He grabbed his coat. It was time for a reunion.

***

Devon packed haphazardly. She needed the first available flight to the States in order to find Dominic as quickly as possible. She knew her suspicions were correct. With a sinking heart, she'd listened as all her calls went to voicemail. Neither of their fathers picked up either. Right now, she couldn't stop to absorb the full meaning of that. There would be time enough on the flight.

She prayed she could stop what Dominic had begun.

Already, it might be too late. The amount of money involved was criminal. Dom would go to jail. Her breath hitched as she jammed her case closed, tangling her clothing in the clasp. After another attempt, she finally clamped it shut and turned, dragging it behind her.

Bennett stood in the doorway.

She cleared her throat, but said nothing. His face was like thunder, and she unconsciously took a step backward.

"Going somewhere?" He snarled the words.

She remained silent, afraid for the first time.

He stepped further into the room and Devon braced herself from taking another step back. He approached, raising a hand. She inwardly berated herself when she minutely flinched.

Black humor curved his lips into a terrible smile. His eyes were dark as pitch.

"Let me help you with that bag."

He jerked it out of her hands. Alarmed, she stared as he opened it, roughly casting aside the contents. He looked up at her, murderously angry.

"Where is it?"

Frightened, bewildered, she blanked. "What?"

"*The MONEY. Goddamn you, where is the money?*"

Whether it was an overload of stress, or pure terror, Devon erupted into hysterical laughter. Could he possibly think *she* had it?

Her mouth snapped shut as Bennett took her shoulders and started shaking her so hard her head jerked back.

Genuinely scared, and angry because of it, she slapped him across the face.

He dropped his hands, walking backwards from her while still staring, intent and furious. Stunned, Devon watched as the imprint of her hand on his cheek whitened, then turned a dull red.

They faced each other, opponents across the room, both breathing hard.

When it became too much, Devon sat, exhausted. "I don't have the money. My God, if I did, it would hardly fit in a suitcase." One last hiccup of laughter escaped before she swallowed it down in the face of his lethal glare.

She winced as he strolled over and ran a hand over her hair in a soft caress. With one finger, he tilted her chin up so she would meet his eyes.

"I thought you were beautiful," he began.

His words were the beginning of every ending she ever feared.

"But you are the ugliest thing a woman can be, Devon. You used your body... and this face," he tapped her cheek, "for the sole purpose of obtaining what you wanted." He pushed her face away with a careless flick. "*Money.* So crass, selling yourself like that. You know what that makes you, don't you?"

Devon froze, betraying nothing. While his words stabbed at her, she wrapped her arms around her middle to hold off the pain. His accusations flayed the skin from her bones, leaving her as a raw mass of screaming nerves.

But she showed none of this. Determined, she relied on the lessons and ways of her past to get her through the present.

She stiffened her back. Rather than answer him, she asked a question of her own. "So was I only a body... a face," she tapped her own cheek this time, "to *you*, Bennett?"

His face flushed. He hissed, "Yes, dammit. *Yes.* It's all you ever were, Devon. It's all you could ever be."

***

The words were such a blatant lie, Bennett worried she might laugh in his face.

He loved her, wildly and fiercely.

Now no matter how it might wound him in the process, he would murder every feeling he had for her. Then, it would be *over*.

Her eyes raked him, interrupting his thoughts. "So you used me, my body."

Aggressive, Bennett nodded in agreement. He'd convince himself, by God, as well as her.

"Then what does that make *you*?"

He stepped forward, incensed, but she stopped him with one hand raised in warning.

"You'll stop right there." He planted his feet. It would already take a lifetime for him to forgive himself for touching her in anger.

"Now tell me what you want."

He whirled around, furious yet unsettled. Inside, he raged, the muscles of his back stiffening until he felt he'd break. Another part of him, a separate part, didn't want her thinking he'd hurt her, no matter the circumstances.

He cursed, pointing at her from across the room. "I want the money back. All of it. You go *nowhere* until you fix this. And tell *Dominic*," he spat the name, "he's going to prison."

"No."

"*What did you say?*"

"No deal. I'll get your money back, but leave Dom out of it. This is between you and me."

It was clear where her loyalties lay. Anguish crushed his chest, widening the ache until it was everywhere.

"Even now, you lie. *Do you even know how to tell the truth?*" Bennett slowly shook his head, outraged with her duplicity.

Pain flashed across her face, then it was gone.

"I know you had his help. For Christ's sake, Devon, he's an Internet and systems security specialist! Did you think I wouldn't put it together?"

She paused, seeming to weigh her options. "Be that as it may, he will remain out of jail. As will everyone involved."

She was calm and it only added to his fury. Before he could speak, she said the rest.

"I will get your money. Your clients will remain unaware this ever happened. *No one* will know you were compromised." She was completely monotone. "Then we'll all go back to our lives."

Disgusted with himself, and her, Bennett stood, fists clenched as he considered her offer. When he was sure he could speak, he replied.

"*Fine*. Except for you, my sweet betrayer. You go back to nothing. Your future is *over*."

CHAPTER FOURTEEN

IN THE EARLY HOURS OF dawn, Devon realized Natalie must be the leak. Focused on finding Dom, worrying about him, had made her skip over the most essential piece of the puzzle. She was the only way he could've obtained the access required to carry out such devastation.

At this point, it hardly mattered whether she'd been a willing participant or not. More importantly, Natalie might know how to reach Dom, and that was more than Devon had accomplished. She'd rang him and both their fathers throughout the night without success.

Devon was starting to panic.

Arriving at Natalie's flat, she loudly banged the knocker. Within minutes, Natalie jerked the door open, glaring.

"*What?*" She hissed the words, belting her robe as she nonetheless stood aside for Devon to enter.

"Believe it or not, I'm sorry to bother you like this. But I'm desperate, and you're my last hope." The words trailed as Devon caught movement out of the corner of her eye. Turning her head, she saw Dominic walking towards them, stretching his arms overhead.

She stormed forward, catching him off guard as she shoved at his chest. Any doubts, or hope, she may have harbored were lost after one look at his face.

He was guilty as sin.

"What the hell?"

He grabbed at her, capturing both of her wrists one-handed. She tried to jerk away, but he held her fast.

"You *snake*. I've been looking all over for you, and I find you here? *Of all places?* Do you know what you've *done*, Dominic?"

"Now just a minute." Natalie interrupted, offense dripping as she took in the drama unfolding within her own home.

Devon rounded on her. "Shut up, Natalie. You're no better. You're lucky to be out of jail, for crying out loud." Devon swung back to Dom. "*You have ruined me.* Both of us, if Bennett has any say."

Natalie looked at her as if she'd gone mad. "What are you talking about?"

"The *money*," Devon answered, sounding exactly as Bennett had. To Dom, she said, "You're going to put it back. *Now*."

He sighed, and the corners of his mouth turned down. "I can't do that."

"You most certainly can. And you will do it, or I might kill you myself." Devon slowed down, making an effort to explain clearly. "I had to pacify Bennett, Dom. He was threatening you with prison time. I promised it would all go back."

Natalie interjected, "What are you two *talking* about?"

They both shouted, in unison. "The *MONEY!*"

Devon heaved a deep breath, praying for calm. "Natalie, I'd say it's apparent you didn't know." She aimed an accusing look at Dom. "But Dominic has hacked Sterling International." She watched as the other woman's eyes went round.

"And he has stolen an *enormous* amount of money."

Natalie groped behind her for a chair, sagging into it.

Devon continued. "Now, I'm going to ensure he keeps the promise I made on his behalf." Two sets of eyes fixed on her, one pair reluctant, the other horrified.

"By putting the money BACK."

***

Dominic tried to reason with Devon, hastily trying to explain the plan was unfinished. Devon cut him off by chopping her hand, slicing the air between them.

"I do not want to hear it. You had every opportunity to explain all this before, and you never said one word. Now, all I care about is that you fix this."

"Devvie, you don't understand. You'd never have allowed—"

Hearing him use her childhood nickname made her grit her teeth. Fighting for control, she murmured, "No, I doubt *you* understand. You've no idea what you've really done, what you've destroyed."

He froze, listening.

"You're still worried about your plan. Your ignorant, destructive scheme. I knew *nothing*. You told me *nothing*. Yet, I was left to clear up your mess." She pushed her hair back from her hot forehead. "You have no idea what it's cost me." Hard eyes met his. "No one would answer my calls. Not you. Not Patrick. Not even my own father."

Dominic spoke quickly. "That was my fault. I told them not to. I was sure I'd reach you in time, before you knew."

Devon looked at him with disgust. Seeing the look, he quietly confessed, albeit reluctantly. "I meant to text you, get you to meet me at Heathrow. But I made a mistake."

Natalie stood abruptly, pushing the chair back in her haste. Devon watched, puzzled, but the other woman strode to the window, turning her back on them.

Devon ground out, "You are supposed to be *my family*. I am not some detail in one of your jobs that needs to be *handled*." Dominic stared helplessly as she smacked her palm on the table. "I *needed* you, any one of you. My *father* wouldn't talk to me, even when I left him message after message." Her voice dropped to a whisper. "I can't count on *any* of you. You left me, abandoned me."

She saw the muscles in his throat work up and down as he took a hard swallow. She was exhausted.

"Please fix it, Dom. I need this to end."

Ultimately, he did as she asked, unable to deny her anymore. As dawn crept into the flat, he finished replacing the last of the funds and erasing any leftover traces of his actions. Natalie still stood near the window, a sentry looking outward. Her posture was iron straight, despite the long hours she'd stood.

Dominic looked up, pushing back from his laptop. "It's done."

Devon closed her eyes, rubbing them with the heels of her palms. Doing so, she missed the quick maneuver where Dominic pocketed a tiny flash drive he'd plugged in earlier, unseen.

She walked to the door, unable to speak to either Dom or Natalie. She turned the knob to leave when Dominic called out.

"Devvie?"

She remained in the doorway, not looking back. "Yes?"

"I'm sorry."

Her shoulders slumped. Stepping forward, she walked out and closed the door quietly behind her.

She was in her car before she pulled out her phone to punch in Bennett's numbers. As his deep voice answered, she echoed Dominic's earlier words.

"It's done." She turned her phone off before he could reply.

***

Bennett stared at his phone.

It's done.

He supposed it was. He ached, hollowed out from the excess of emotions.

He needed some peace.

He'd have someone, at work and his home, box her things and courier them to her flat. He wanted no reminders.

This way, he would never see her again.

Rubbing his chest, he walked to the shower. He was meeting his grandfather today, maybe that would help take his mind off her. But first, he'd go into the office, finish things. The idea didn't bring the relief he expected, just a dull throbbing headache.

It's done.

***

As Natalie stood like a statue, numb, Dom took the liberty of showering and changing. He obviously needed to be somewhere, somewhere other than with her. He set his bag down by the door and crossed to her.

"Toff."

The ice began to crack. "Don't call me that."

She'd turned all the possibilities over in her mind, recalling their relationship since its first day. No matter how she rotated it, the light refused to brighten his actions.

"Did you take my password?" Her voice was listless. There was no other way he could've done what he had. He'd needed someone inside.

"Yes."

She'd been a fool. He'd used her, but she allowed it. Every step of the way.

"I have to leave now, but I'd like to come back. Explain."

Finally, she turned her head to look at him. He could have been one of the ancient gods, with his burnished gold hair and mossy eyes glinting in the early morning light.

She'd remember him this way, beautiful and masculine except for his deceptive, lying lips.

"Go, Dominic. And never, ever come back."

She waited until his steps faded away before allowing the first tears to fall.

She wept for all she'd lost, and everything she had yet to lose that day.

***

Bennett wandered through his outer offices, wondering where Natalie could be. In all their years working together, she'd never been late, not once.

His brow creased. She was never sick, either. Considering that, he decided to bump her pay. It was past time to stop taking her for granted.

Considering the hell of the past few days, he had a strong appreciation for loyalty.

He settled at his desk, looking up when his door opened moments later. Expecting to see his PA, he was shocked speechless to see Dominic Martin strolling in. Bennett's jaw clenched. The other man continued, nonchalantly plopping down in a chair facing him.

Dominic silently scanned the décor.

"You have a damn nerve showing up here. You're lucky I don't have you thrown in jail." Bennett grated the words, unable to believe the man's gall.

Still, Dominic looked around, taking it all in. He reached out to run an admiring hand over the edges of Bennett's desk.

"Mm. A classic Partner's desk. Regency?" He didn't wait for an answer. "Yes. And gorgeous serpentine burlwood." He glanced up. "You have excellent taste."

"What the hell do you care about my desk, my office? Are you casing the place?"

Dom threw back his head, laughing.

Bennett glared, clearly not amused.

Sobering, Dominic got to the point. "I'm here on business."

"Are you *joking*? You are unbelievable."

"I ask that you keep an open mind, Mr. Sterling. We seem to have gotten our wires crossed, and I'll take the blame for that."

"Oh, I'm *Mr. Sterling*, am I? Why the formality? After all, we're practically old acquaintances, considering the fact *you stole my clients' money.*" The words dripped with sarcasm as Bennett seethed. "Hell, you stole *my* money."

"Well yes. But I had to do that, you see."

Bennett shifted back in his seat. He would personally throw him out in a minute. "Go on. *This* I have to hear."

"It was the best and most efficient way of illustrating to you the weakness in your network. Really, it was better for me to steal it than someone else. After all, I was always going to put it back."

Bennett laughed, long and hard. "You were going to put it back. *Right.*" He rose, straightening to his full height. "I've heard enough of your fairytales. Now leave."

Dominic placed a folder on the desk, sliding it across with a careless push. "Before I do, why don't you have a look?"

Something in Dominic's manner intrigued him despite his simmering irritation. Curious, Bennett sat, flipping open the folder. Inside was a completed evaluation of his data security systems with risk analysis of weaknesses, ranked by level of perceived threat and estimated associated loss. Several minutes passed while he continued to read the report, including the proposal for a Martin Security Systems installation with state of the art firewalls and advanced protection from cybercriminals.

He closed the report, resting his chin on steepled fingers.

"You want to contract for my business."

"Yes."

"You arranged an elaborate scheme just so you could work with me."

"I planned a project that would enable me to showcase my unique skills. In turn, you received a firsthand demonstration of your vulnerabilities. You also received the reassurance that we can fix anything, given the remote chance anything should go wrong."

"You're a hacker."

"I used to be. Yes." Dom was unapologetic.

Bennett blew out a long breath. He knew people. And he recognized genius when it was presented to him within a shiny bound folder across his desk.

"I don't like you. I sure as hell don't trust you," he began. Dominic waited. "But as much as I hate it, you're impressive."

"You don't have to like me. You'll learn to trust me. And I *am* impressive." Dominic baldly stated the facts. "Let me show you what I can do for your company."

"You can *never* pull another stunt like this." In spite of himself, Bennett liked Dominic's brash confidence. The other man was certainly charismatic. "We'll work out the details of a trial contract." He held up a finger as Dominic's mouth tilted in a grin.

"A *trial* contract. If you're as good as you say, I'll extend the length of it."

"Fair enough. I look forward to working with you, Mr. Sterling."

"Call me Bennett." He raked his gaze over Dominic. "You certainly are persuasive, but we'll see if you can hold up your end of things *without* the inside help."

Dominic froze, capturing Bennett's attention. "I don't know what you mean."

"Don't bother to deny it now," Bennett interrupted. "You couldn't have accomplished what you did without Devon's help. I hope you're giving *her* a job."

Dominic's face cleared as Bennett spoke. Then he frowned, clearly confused. "Devon didn't help me."

It was Bennett's turn to go still.

"And why would I hire Devvie? She's an economist."

***

Bennett was going to be late.

After settling Dominic into a cab outside, he returned to find Natalie at her desk, unloading her laptop and a hefty stack of file folders.

"Natalie, there you are. I worried you were ill. But then, you're never sick are you?"

She continued unpacking her straining bag, pale behind perfect makeup.

"Your absence this morning made me realize you were due for a raise. I've arranged a package for you in Human Resources." At her continued silence, he said, "I want you to know how much I value you. Personally and professionally."

She leveled a look of quiet devastation at him. She quickly dropped her eyes again, holding out a heavy bond envelope with Bennett's name written on it in neat script.

He raised a brow.

"It's my resignation, Bennett. I was the leak."

No.

Natalie gathered her coat around her and walked out, not looking back. Minutes ticked by as Bennett stood immobile, still holding the letter. It was too much with everything else. Shock piled on top of surprise, one thing after another.

His phone pinged, reminding him he was late.

Laying the envelope down, he decided to table its contents and Natalie's accompanying confession until later.

He'd had enough.

He hurried through the pathways of the City's cemetery, eager to meet his grandfather. Granddad's support was unwavering and he could do with a strong shoulder.

It was a blustery, cold day, perfectly suited to Bennett's mood.

He rounded the final corner to find Charles sitting on a bench, bundled up while gazing toward the grave of his late wife. He held a bouquet of white roses.

Bennett slowed to a stop. Charles waved him over to sit beside him.

A comfortable silence enveloped them. Bennett felt some of the tension leave him as he relaxed against the seat.

His last time here had been with Devon. Memories assailed him. Her beautiful face. Her hair. How she'd held his hand right near this spot.

"Hello grandson. How are you doing?"

After leaving here that day, he'd surprised her with the train trip to Devon. A romantic beginning to a magical weekend.

It's done.

There was no going back. Not after the things he'd said to her, the vile accusations he'd leveled.

He glanced up, aware his grandfather was looking at him with concern. He had no idea what Charles had said.

"Excuse me?" Bennett's voice was rough, strained.

"Never mind. Why don't you tell me what's wrong?"

He'd loved his grandfather all his life, had hoped to emulate him by becoming half as good a man. His smile was self-deprecating.

It's done.

"I did the unforgivable. I had something. It was pure and good. But fragile." Sadness radiated from him. "In my anger and mistrust, I took that fragility and crushed it, shattering it to pieces." A vision assaulted him; Devon's hair tumbling as he'd shaken her. "With ugly words and ugly deeds."

Charles was watching him, nothing but kindness in his eyes. "You're in love."

"I was. I *am*. And I think she loved me until I destroyed it." He choked to a halt.

"You think you've killed her feeling for you?"

"I know I did."

It's done.

"How perfect we should be here." Charles stood to walk to his wife's headstone, touching the granite with the ease of long familiarity. "Bennett, do you think love is easy?"

Bennett raised his head, watching his grandfather trace the words etched into the marble.

Love Everlasting

"I suppose not."

"Let me assure you it is not. But when love's the real thing, it rises above its own ashes. It lasts, on and on, because it is stronger than the things we do in our endless carelessness to harm it."

Bennett's head throbbed as he stared at the words.

Love Everlasting

Was it possible? Could Devon forgive his callousness?

Could he have another chance with her? Show her he was stronger, and wiser, for losing her?

Charles resumed his seat, seemingly content with silence as hope began to unfurl within Bennett.

Long minutes later, his gaze drifted to the bouquet of red roses lying on top of Rose's gravestone. He was amazed he hadn't noticed.

"I thought you only brought Nan white roses."

"I do. But a young lady stopped by with these earlier, saying that a Rose shouldn't be without flowers, even in winter." Bennett sprung up to inspect the bouquet for a card, a message, anything. He missed Charles' self-satisfied smile.

"What did she look like?"

Charles adopted an offhand air. "She was quite stunning. Tall with dark, mink brown hair. But it was her eyes that stood out."

Bennett prodded him. "Yes? Granddad, what was it about her eyes?"

"They were colorless as mist. Nearly clear, like glass."

In his eagerness, Bennett failed to recognize the words he'd used months ago to describe Devon to Charles.

"Quite stunning. And smart with it."

Bennett sat back down, leaning towards his grandfather. "Did she talk to you?"

"Yes, and it was rather profound, I must say. As she laid her roses down, she said that innocence had its place, but a woman wanted to be loved, fully and passionately."

Hoarse, Bennett asked, "Was that all?"

"No. She said one other thing."

Bennett waited, anxious.

"Although pretty, pedestals were lonely places to be. And the fall could be a long one."

CHAPTER FIFTEEN

DEVON ESCAPED.

It was simple, in the end. She packed her suitcases then resolutely discarded whatever didn't fit.

She didn't want to think about giving away the little cat figurine to her neighbor, along with other odds and ends. Even though she'd carried it with her all these years, it was time to let go. The time for sentiment was past.

She needed to accept that some things, some people, were not for her.

I can never have Bennett Sterling.

She pressed her hand over her heart, soothing an invisible wound.

Shutting the door on her flat, she said goodbye to London. Already, she'd gone to the bank and liquidated funds into cash. Booking a flight under a false name hadn't worried her as she had the fake identification to support it. She'd gotten them on a lark during college, for a little gambling con she and Dominic cooked up.

And they were good, so she'd recklessly kept them. Even when she'd sworn to move from the shadows of her past, she hadn't entirely walked away. Not if she were honest.

She was going to break the law.

Paying cash would afford anonymity from credit card traces. With little doubt Dominic could mine her movements through her passport she opted for the alias. Even after weighing the risk, she chose to gamble against being caught. She needed solitude and time. And she would take it.

Bennett already tarred her as a criminal, a thief. She'd live up to his accusations by running so far from him and her family; they'd never find her.

At least not for a while.

She would have her space, and time, to heal.

Two hours later, she boarded her plane to Atlanta, Georgia. From there, she'd move on to Savannah, a city that never failed to comfort her. She dumped her cell phone into an airport trash receptacle, right before the gate.

There. No one would be able to reach her.

Just like she'd been unable to reach them.

As the plane climbed into the darkened sky and headed across the Atlantic, she leaned her head back, hurting.

I will never have Bennett Sterling.

*** ***

Bennett ushered John Sinclair into his office, where Dominic and Patrick Martin waited. He recognized traces of Devon in her father's mannerisms, but it was his eyes that robbed Bennett of breath. They were the palest, misty gray.

God, he missed her.

He was going mad without her.

He'd gone after her that day, now weeks ago. He'd rushed to her flat, ready to plead. The words had trembled on his lips.

I'm sorry.

I love you.

Please forgive me.

But she was gone. Desperate to set things right, he'd knocked on her neighbor's door. Devon had liked the older woman, checking in with her frequently.

Sadly, the woman explained Ms. Sinclair had moved all her things out. She didn't expect her to be back.

Scarcely able to believe it, he'd listened in horror.

"She packed her suitcases and gave the rest of her things away." She shook her head. "She was upset, I could tell. She wasn't crying but it was almost like—"

"What? Tell me, please. It's important."

"It was like she was grieving."

Bennett's gut clenched.

"She gave me this to remember her by," she picked up a tiny porcelain kitten.

Bennett recognized it. One day, Devon had shown him all her odds and ends, as she called them. She'd been very fond of the little statue; she'd had it since she was young. At the time, her father told her it was the closest thing to a real cat she'd get.

"I tried to make her take it back, but she wouldn't. Said it was time to let some things go." The older woman carefully replaced the kitten on her mantle. "I could tell it was a wrench for her. I hope she'll come back for it. I told her she could."

In the end, he'd walked out of her apartment with the tiny ceramic piece cradled in his pocket. Explaining that it was important, he'd promised to return it to Devon, who he was sure would be sorry she'd left it behind.

Unfortunately, the figurine still lay nestled in tissue, boxed and wrapped in the glove box of his car. A week later he'd bought her another gift that waited in his townhouse.

He'd given her neither.

He couldn't *find* her.

His new PA brought in coffees, interrupting his gloomy thoughts. Dominic's eyes darted to the door as it opened, before quickly dropping to his clenched hands.

Natalie was gone too.

"I need help," Bennett announced. "I've looked everywhere. I've hired people to look further. I'm starting to think she's left the UK, but I don't see how as she hasn't used her passport."

A lightning glance passed between the other three men.

"We've been searching for her too, with no luck." It was John that spoke up. "She's covered her tracks, probably using an assumed—"

Dominic shifted, nudging John with a subtle elbow.

Bennett zeroed in on the movement. "John? You were saying?"

Clear eyes met his. "Nothing, nothing."

Bennett raised a brow.

John cleared his throat. "Devvie's very resourceful, that's all. And smart as a tack, as you know."

Dominic leaned forward, staring down at the table they were gathered round. He spoke.

"She's hurting. She'll want to be alone, and she'll make sure she is." Keeping his head down, he shot side glances at John and Patrick. "Dev felt rejected by us when we wouldn't take her calls. It's the worst thing we could have done to her."

John Sinclair sighed, suddenly looking closer to his actual age. "You're right, Dom. She fears abandonment. She never got over Angeline's desertion."

"Her mother?" Bennett grabbed at the information, greedy to know more. She'd closed him off, but he hadn't seen it at the time.

"Yes. For all of five minutes, Angeline was Devon's mother." Bitterness turned the corners of John's mouth down. "She left us when Dev was hardly old enough to remember her."

"I'd say she remembered Angeline very well," Bennett murmured. "And the legacy she left behind."

There was silence as the four men digested their guilt. They'd all let her down, each in their own way.

"Right." As Bennett spoke, three heads turned back to him. "So the question is: where the *hell* is she?"

A din erupted, each man throwing out ideas for where she might have gone. Despite the circumstances, Bennett couldn't help but be reluctantly amused. They were a band of men, bonded into brotherhood through family and loyal friendship.

Because of his love for Devon, he now belonged too.

Eventually, they left, each off on their individual missions to locate her. Bennett stood at the window, his earlier amusement gone. As the lights of London began winking on in the twilight, a profound loneliness settled in.

His office door opened. Aidan entered, tossing a report down on Bennett's desk.

"Where the hell *is* Devon? What did you do to send her away this time?"

He could admit his crimes to himself. Share a slice with Devon's family. But he wouldn't be baring his soul to staff, not even Aidan. "Excuse me?"

Aidan flipped a few pages of the report, jabbing his fingers on a graph. "It took me a full day to calculate what she'd do in a few hours." He glared up into Bennett's face. "I'm still not sure I didn't make a mistake. But Devon never made errors. She was the best economist you ever had, and you drove her off."

Bennett heaved a breath, scowling. "Are you finished?"

Aidan paled, but remained standing tall. Bennett knew his face must look like thunder, but he couldn't talk about her with Aidan.

Not anyone. Since she left, he was too raw with wanting and needing her.

"I miss her. She was my colleague, but a friend too."

"I know. I miss her too," Bennett admitted.

Aidan was visibly surprised. "You mean you *want* her to come back?"

God yes.

"Yes. I'd tell her if I could find her. But she's disappeared."

Bennett sat, wearily running a hand through his hair.

Aidan remained standing. "You have no idea where she's gone?"

Bennett shook his head, unable to say more. But Aidan had other ideas, expectantly waiting for Bennett's explanation.

Running a hand over the stubble on his jaw, Bennett chose his words carefully. "She was upset. I said some terrible things to her, thinking she was involved with the theft."

"You suspected *Devon?*" Aidan was perplexed. "Bennett, she's more loyal than anyone I've ever known. She wouldn't betray you. She couldn't."

"No, but I betrayed her. I had no faith in her. No trust." The sympathy in Aidan's kindly gaze made sharing easier. "Now it's too late. I have no idea where she would go at a time like this."

He lowered his head into his hands, staring at the report with its rows of meaningless data. Aidan carefully seated himself across from him. As Bennett prepared to send him on his way, Aidan spoke.

"I'll leave you in a minute, but first hear me out."

Something in the other man's tone had Bennett's head shooting up in attention.

"I think *I* know where she could be."

***

Bennett found her amongst the graves in Savannah, lying below the massive oaks that wept with Spanish moss. She sat on a blanket, eyes closed, dappled with late winter sun.

At his cautious approach, misty gray eyes opened to stare into his.

His breath locked. Taking a minute, he soaked her in. She could be an apparition, lying among the mildewed stones around her. But she looked fragile, brittle almost.

She'd lost weight.

Bennett's chest tightened. "Hello, Devon."

She squeezed her eyes shut then opened them again. Careful to keep some inches away, he sat beside her, holding a massive bouquet of red roses. His hands itched to touch her, but he didn't want her to run from him. Not ever again.

"I'm sorry."

Long moments passed where he feared she wouldn't answer. When she did, he inwardly winced.

"Why are you here, Bennett? Didn't you say everything the last time we were together? Or did you leave out another horrible accusation?"

He repeated himself. "I'm sorry, so sorry." He'd say it a hundred, or a thousand times if needed. He'd say it all their lives, if she'd have him back.

She shuddered, arms crossing her stomach. "I don't want you to be sorry. I want you to go."

"No. I'd do anything for you. But I will *not* leave you again."

"That's all I want from you. To go. It was peaceful here, and now you're ruining it." The words were wrenched from her, and Bennett could hear the underlying hurt driving her on.

"I made a mistake, Devon. An indefensible, horrible mistake. But I have to believe we can get past it. I need you back."

She picked up some fallen leaves and systematically began shredding them. Finally, she raised her eyes to meet his. "There wouldn't be any point. Please go. I know you're hurting too, but this doesn't help either one of us. We were never meant to be, Bennett."

"Don't say that," his stomach clenched, defending him against injury.

"No, I have to. So we can both move on." Her face was pinched, but determined. His heart dropped.

"You kept me on a pedestal. Told me I was perfect. Always, in every way. But I'm not perfect, not even close. And when I fell from your impossible expectations, you crucified me."

He swallowed, hard. "I don't want a perfect ideal. I want *you*."

"You don't mean that, not really. It would only be a matter of time before I disappointed you again." She laughed without humor. "My God, you cannot imagine what kind of family I have. Who I really am."

"I've met your family, we've been working together to find you. I *like* them. I know who you are, Devon. And I love you. I'll love you for the rest of my life."

She turned her head away, smoothing the blanket with unsteady fingers.

"I don't believe you."

Bennett changed tack. He'd come this far; he could be patient. "Why are you here, Devon? Why cemeteries?"

She looked around. "Savannah is where we lived when my mother left us," she began. "I couldn't understand it. I waited for her to come back, but she never did." Vulnerable gray eyes met his. He'd never loved her more. "With a child's logic, I decided she must have died, and my father refused to tell me." She gave a small ironic smile. "We are great liars, as you know by now."

Bennett couldn't return her black humor. Too much was riding on his every word, every action. He waited.

"Every chance I got, I came here, to find her. This cemetery. I searched and searched, a girl walking through the graves, looking for her mother's name on the stones." She was quiet for a moment. "And then one day, I realized she *hadn't* died. She'd really left us." She shredded another leaf. "For once, my dad told the truth." She laughed, darkly. "But by then, I'd developed a fondness." She waved a hand, encompassing the area. "This place is constant. It's unchanging and sure." She dusted her hands off. "I like it."

She was breaking his heart.

Reaching into his pocket, he produced a small box and sat it in her lap.

"Marry me."

She wouldn't touch the box, just stared down at it like he'd tossed a viper at her.

"I love you. Marry me."

She jumped up, tumbling the box to the ground. "Haven't you listened to a word I've said?"

"I listened, but it's my turn now. I love you. I know I hurt you, horribly. I'll spend the rest of our lives making that up to you if you'll let me."

She scorched him with contempt. "You didn't hurt me. You lived up to expectations, that's all." At his puzzled frown, she continued. "You left. People leave. It's no big deal," she cried. "I don't want this. I don't want *you*. Please repeat what you did so well before. *Leave*."

She spun around, pacing away. She was practically bleeding out her hurt. Her distress wounded him as well, but it was now or never. The chasm of pain and damage he'd caused must be crossed. It was *his* turn to show faith, when before he'd had none.

He walked to her. Reaching for the box, he opened it toward her as he knelt on a bed of leaves.

"Marry me."

She glanced at it, caught. Her look told Bennett everything he needed to know. The perpetual ache around his heart eased at last.

Unconsciously, she stepped nearer. Shyly curious, she absorbed the brilliant oval cut diamond with its halo of smaller stones set in rose gold.

Her eyes leapt to his.

"*No*."

Mortally wounded, Bennett held his uncomfortable position on the ground. So much was at stake. He had to make her see him. Accept him.

"You left *me*." His throat ached.

"What?"

"I failed you, utterly. But rather than stay and fight, you left. The abandoned became the abandoner. What kind of love doesn't forgive, Devon?"

Tears flooded her eyes and she angrily swiped them away. "I don't love you."

"You do." He gently destroyed her. "Don't lie, not about this."

She crumpled to the ground, too fast for Bennett to scramble towards her. She dissolved into tears, great wracking sobs that shook her slender frame. He sank down next to her, enfolding her into his arms. He held her as she cried it all out, releasing the pain and anger she'd held locked inside. Finally, she quieted, sagging against him.

He tipped her chin up. Charcoal dark eyes swirled to foggy gray.

"I love you, Devon Sinclair. Will you do me the honor of becoming my wife?"

She hiccuped, one last sob escaping her. Alarmed, Bennett asked, "I can never be sorry enough for what I said. Forgive me?"

She raised her lips to his, silencing his worries. Soothing.

"I do, Bennett." She shushed him before he could speak, pressing another soft kiss on his mouth.

"I was too hurt to admit I still loved you. I doubted your feelings for me — that they'd be strong enough to survive what happened. I never trusted you to stay, so I left at the first opportunity that proved me right." She toyed with one of his buttons.

Bennett removed another box, similarly wrapped as the first, from his pocket.

Giving it a cursory glance, she raised shiny eyes to his. "Yes."

"Yes?"

"Yes, I'll marry you." She beamed a watery smile.

Bennett grabbed for the first box, taking the ring out to slip onto her finger. It was a perfect fit.

Bemused, she stared at it. "You got the size right. Again."

"The most important one. Now open your other present."

Because she hadn't really looked before, he knew she'd thought it was the ring box. Now, she picked the second one up, rotating the box around as she inspected it. Excitement sparked in her eyes as a blush stained her cheeks.

Bennett grinned, realizing Devon had a weakness for gifts. He'd make sure to exploit that for the next fifty years or so.

"What is it?"

"Open it and see."

She untied the ribbon and carefully removed the lid. She stared at the porcelain figurine of the little white cat, timelessly caught in the act of napping. She cradled it to her chest. "Oh, God. You got it back for me."

"I did. And I got you a real one too." He hitched his chin at the kitten. "Although he might be grown by the time you decide to come back to me."

She bowled him over, kissing his face from top to bottom. He brought her lips to his even as he laughed, desire igniting in a mixture of love and passion.

She cupped his face. "Thank you. Thank you for loving me enough to find me."

"Devon, I would have searched for you until the day I died. You're the one for me." He kissed her forehead, pulling her up to stand. "From the very beginning, it was you. There could be no other."

Later, as they walked through the old Savannah cemetery, Devon pointed out favorite grave markers and statues to Bennett. One of the last had cherubs looking upward, stretching to eternity while their hands twined, forever linked. He paused to touch it, pulling a bloom from the bouquet she carried.

Shaking his head at Devon's puzzled look, he laid the red rose on the granite. Below it, the inscription read:

Love Everlasting

Taking Devon's hand, he walked with her to the exit. A new beginning and the rest of their lives awaited.

***

Devon stretched, comfortably ensconced in first class next to Bennett. As the plane glided over the Atlantic, she watched him sleep. His face was relaxed, the grooves he'd acquired in the weeks before smoothing out.

He loosely held her hand, even in slumber. He'd barely let her out of his sight for the past week.

With enough time, he'd accept that she'd never leave him. Not ever again.

She raised her other hand to admire her engagement ring in the faint light of the cabin.

I have Bennett Sterling. And he has me.

When she'd thought all was lost, he'd come for her. He always would.

They'd failed each other, forgetting themselves in the ordeal of Dominic's scheme. But in losing what they had, they'd emerged stronger. Truer.

Her lips curved in a small, secret smile. She shouldn't have doubted them.

After all, Devon Sinclair never failed a test.

And apparently, neither did Bennett Sterling.

THE END

A Note From Kat

I'd like to sincerely thank you for reading about Devon and Bennett in *A Matter of Trust,* Book One in my *London Calling* series. If you enjoyed their story and want to know more about what comes next with Natalie and Dominic, and what *really* happened with Angeline, then I would love for you to sign up at http://www.katfaitour.com for all my upcoming news, book releases and free content.

Finally, if you loved the book, it would do me a great service if you were to leave a short review on Amazon or Goodreads. Your assistance in recommending the book spreads the word to new readers and helps others find my series.

Thank you!

Kat Faitour
http://www.katfaitour.com

About Kat Faitour

I write about modern, sexy characters in fabulous settings. No matter what, romance is always guaranteed in my emotionally punchy, smart, and passionate stories.

My lifelong love affair with books began at the age of three when my brother taught me to read. It was an ambitious undertaking, since he was only five. He always made sure I kept up with what he was reading, which meant I missed out on books by Dr. Seuss in favor of those by J.R.R. Tolkien and Anne McCaffrey.

Unfortunately for my brother (and fortunately for me), I was introduced to romance as a young teen and nothing has been the same since. While I still read his fantasy and fiction picks, my passion always brings me back to romances with compelling emotional stories.

Alas, my brother believes me to be a libertine, abandoning the realms of higher genre fiction to wallow in sexy stories about beautiful people in gorgeous places.

I suppose he's right. But I remind him all the best stories are adventures. And what better adventure than two people finding each other, learning to love, and spending their lives together?

Made in the USA
Lexington, KY
28 May 2016